A
Literary
Woman

A
Literary
Woman

MARY BECKETT

BLOOMSBURY

First published 1990
Copyright © 1990 by Mary Beckett

Bloomsbury Publishing Ltd, 2 Soho Square, London W1V 5DE

A CIP catalogue record for this book is available
from the British Library

ISBN 0 7475 0607 8

10 9 8 7 6 5 4 3 2 1

Some of the stories in this collection have been previously published as follows: 'The Long Engagement' (*In Dublin*); 'A Ghost Story', 'Inheritance' and 'Under Control' (*Irish Press*); and 'Heaven' (*Wildish Things*, Attic Press, 1989).

Photoset by Rowland Phototypesetting Ltd,
Bury St Edmunds, Suffolk
Printed and bound in Great Britain by
Butler and Tanner Ltd, Frome and London

There are no secrets in Ireland, it is said, but there is a sinister presence in this collection of stories who is prepared to wreck lives in the pursuit of these secrets . . .

A dilatory bachelor extends his bitter-sweet engagement for just too long. A newly-wed couple discovers something more fundamental needs to be exorcised from their marriage than the wailing phantom in their haunted house. An independent woman is appalled to learn she has inherited a fierce commitment to motherhood. Bossiness receives an intriguing defence, the painful anxieties and guilt of parenthood are exposed, and an innocent addiction to peace and quiet gives rise to nasty suspicion.

Meanwhile, the anonymous 'watcher' taunts her neighbours with viperous communications. The separate lives depicted in Mary Beckett's supremely well-crafted stories are linked by a common nuisance. What they reveal about life in Ireland – North and South – about families everywhere, about the oppression of love and the balm of peace, is rarely so eloquently expressed. Following her acclaimed first novel, *Give Them Stones*, Mary Beckett's new collection is a welcome and invigorating successor.

CONTENTS

A
Literary
Woman

The Long Engagement

The Long Engagement

The big high-ceilinged room where Judy lived was cold when she arrived in from work, and she had just plugged in her electric fire when the phone rang down in the hall. It had never been accepted that she had any right to answer the phone unless the widow and her family who owned the house were out. So she stood, still wearing her coat, listening.

In all the years since she had left her warm family home in Belfast for a job in Dublin she had never acclimatised herself to the chill of this house. There were times at the beginning when homesickness tempted her to resign and take the next train north. Her own pride and her parents' pride in her prevented that. 'She's running the civil service for them up there,' her mother, beaming, told the neighbours, and even her undemonstrative father smiled at her when she arrived home for the holidays, and shook hands with her. Her brothers and sisters, trying in vain for his approval, complained that only people who left home were appreciated. They had all left home in their own time and Belfast had receded. For a few years she shared the room with another girl, and they had laughed at all the oddities and inconveniences, but the girl went off to get married and the stiffness came back.

There was a ladylike tap on the door and Mrs Robinson said, 'Miss Brennan – telephone.' On the way downstairs, Judy thought, 'It's Martin to tell me he isn't coming for me tonight,' and her hello was distant.

'Judy, is that you? You don't sound like yourself. I'll call for you at half-past seven. Is that all right? We'll go to Dun Laoire – I have something to tell you. I thought maybe you'd like to know so you'd put on your best dress.'

She didn't feel any pleasure until she was back in her room. The first mistaken mood of misery persisted after it should have been dispersed by the phone call. She filled the kettle for a cup of tea and stood looking at her cactus on the window-ledge. It was small, grey-green, insignificant. She had bought it at a bring-and-buy sale from the schoolgirl daughter of her former flatmate. The girl had told her it would grow big and flower. Until a week ago it had done nothing at all except give Judy a sore finger when she touched it accidentally. Then one of its little spiny bumps in the middle of the fleshy pad began to swell. Every day it was bigger, and now this evening she noticed that another little knob had grown out of the first one. Judy found herself smiling. 'It's an omen,' she thought.

The one-bar electric fire warmed her legs and the tea warmed her throat. She settled for little areas of comfort because always the prospect of marrying Martin kept her from trying to make the flat more habitable. There was a huge fireplace, so on really cold evenings she could light a fire. At other times all the draughts in the room converged on the chimney. When Judy heard people talking of good old-fashioned solidly built houses she wondered did they really exist. This house looked solid from outside, substantial, three-storeyed, with granite steps up to an elegant fan-lighted door in the middle floor. Inside there were gaps between the floor and skirting boards. The electric wiring was plainly visible down these gaps. Every autumn mice invaded her room and she had to set traps night after night. She had to buy new traps day after day because she never undid the dead mouse. She could not bear to look at the tiny animal with one bright eye open towards her and the soft grey fur only slightly marked where the trap had caught it. She felt cruel to kill such harmless-looking things but she still had the horror of scurrying feet and gnawing teeth in the darkness. She kept not only all her food in the fridge, since it was the only place safe from their dirt, but her own cup and saucer, plates and cutlery too. Martin's bungalow was snug, tight, new – at least it was new when Judy met Martin first and was brought home to meet his mother.

From the first night they met, his mother adopted her as an ally. When Martin opened the door under the stairs to hang up her coat Mrs Corrigan insisted on showing Judy. 'Look at the way it is! Everybody else has this all fitted out as a cloakroom, with panelling and hooks and a mirror and shelves, but what do we do? We still hang our coats on the three nails banged into the stairs by the builders to hang *their* coats on. I'm always at Martin to fix it up, and he's always going to, but there it is.' Judy smiled at Martin – she was always smiling at Martin. He didn't appear to mind what his mother said. He treated her tenderly as indeed he always treated Judy. The good humour in his warm brown eyes never failed.

Mrs Corrigan formed the habit of telephoning Judy when Martin was out. She mentioned on each occasion that Martin *was* out. She then gave a monologue on the theme of Martin and what Judy must do about Martin, while Judy stood in the Robinsons' draughty hall wondering was she taking an undue time at the phone.

'He's an only child of elderly parents, so you'll just have to accept that he hasn't much drive. Things have to be decided for him and he has to be pushed. All he wanted to do when he left school was run the farm – only a small little bit of a farm, mind you. His father was content with it, but if it hadn't been for my pay as a teacher we'd have had few comforts. It was no life for any young man to settle for, but even when he was teaching in Dublin nothing would do him but come home every weekend to keep the farm going. The only thing I could do eventually was sell up – my husband left everything to me of course – and buy this bungalow here. And he's happy here. He's a very happy person, don't you think? I'm very proud of him. So you'll have to take over from me, Judy, and look after him very well.'

'Not a bit scruffy – you'd certainly never take him for a national teacher,' Judy's friends used to say, admiring his lean figure in his expensive suits. She learned that his suits never wore out – that he had had some of them for years. She wondered was it because he moved so deliberately. His auburn hair had no trace of grey and the long wrinkle from his cheekbone to his jaw was no deeper now than when Judy first loved to rub her own pink firm face against it.

Now she laid out the expensive cosmetics that she used every day to ward off the signs of age. They depressed her when she examined her reflection in direct sunlight. Sometimes she saw in the mirror her mother's ruined prettiness. Sometimes her father's bleak eyes gazed back at her. She would be ridiculous as a bride, she told herself repeatedly, and still she could not face the thought that she would never be one. She had not been especially interested in having children when she thought it was inevitable, but now that it would soon be impossible she felt humiliated. It would be easy to hate Martin when he wasn't there looking at her fondly, but at all times there was the attraction of the bungalow.

He kept house efficiently. During the year following his mother's death and his formal engagement to Judy she was not at the bungalow very often. Martin said they mustn't give rise to gossip. He lived in the parish in which he taught, so he insisted he must be careful. When he asked her to the house it was with other friends. The first thing she noticed was the cloakroom under the stairs beautifully fitted out. She had thought then that he had done it in preparation for her, and she had admired the ring on her finger and felt happy and secure. But the year ended without any definite word of a wedding day. At first Judy brought up the subject, but Martin was evasive. After each mention there would be a longer silence from him when he didn't ring her or write to her and she was terrified that he'd dropped her and mortified at her terror. When she did see him again she was so pleased and so tempted to put her hands on his hair and on his face that they never quarrelled.

Her friends tried to tell her that she should break it off, that there was no future in it. They suggested some place more comfortable to live, perhaps even a small house. She couldn't even make herself buy a record player because it would be an admission that she didn't expect to get married soon. Just after his mother's death Martin had bought one and he invited his friends in to listen to his records. Judy acted as hostess and when he had delicately placed the needle on his chosen track he'd sit down beside her on the couch and deliberately drop his arm on her shoulders. She could never accustom herself to conversation during the music. If she had to talk, the music was an irritation. If she listened to the music she couldn't think of what people were saying. Sometimes she detached herself smilingly from Martin's comradely arm and sat on a stool apart, leaning her head back against Martin's living-room wall with her eyes closed, listening. Now and again she felt such exhilaration that neither Martin nor loneliness mattered at all. Last year Martin had bought a new compact-disc player.

She opened her door and stepped out on the landing, watching for the whereabouts of the Robinsons, before going up the short flight of stairs to the bathroom. The youngest girl was studying in the attic, learning aloud. The only access to her attic was through the bathroom, so Judy could never have a bath without checking first that she wouldn't want in or out. Only late at night when the girl had gone to bed could Judy relax in her bath without feeling she was a restriction on the Robinsons – and by that time the water was cold. The bath sat on big claw feet. The surface was rough. Sometimes the Robinson girls painted it with enamel paint but it never seemed to dry out properly. Judy shivered as she knelt in the shallow water and leaned over to wash her face. Then her soapy hands briskly rubbing her breasts felt the lump.

The dark-blue bathroom tilted and whirled round. She dropped her hands and put her chin down hard on her chest. 'It's not so,' she told herself when her sight cleared, 'I imagined it.' And she stayed as she was while the water cooled. Then she forced herself to explore what she had found, though her stomach was sick as if she had to touch some loathsome thing. In the badly lighted room without her glasses she could see nothing, but her qualmish fingers found at the side of her breast under her arm a solid lump firmly fixed under the skin with, she thought, other little excrescences from it. 'I'll go to the doctor. He'll tell me it's nothing,' she whispered, her mouth dry. There was a knock on the attic door. 'Will you be long, Miss Brennan? I've to go out to a debate,' the Robinson girl said apologetically, and Judy quickly dried herself, put on her dressing-gown and let the girl through. Afterwards she cleaned up carefully and went back to her own room. The mirror showed her face very white. She mocked at herself.

'Such a fuss about nothing.' She dabbed her lipstick at her cheekbones and blended in the pink. For once she was glad of the extra twenty minutes before Martin rang the front doorbell. He was always late, sometimes ten minutes, sometimes as much as half an hour.

'You are looking well,' Martin greeted her. 'I am always proud to be seen with you.' Judy was dizzy for a moment at the top of the steep steps and needed his courteous hand at her elbow, but he noticed nothing.

The restaurant was dimly lit. Purple candles flickered on each pink damasked table. Martin was confident, ordering lobster bisque and prawn curry. Judy was never interested in rich foods; she had been reared in a household where dinner was meat, potatoes and vegetables, soup if the day was cold and dessert on Sundays. These expensive appurtenances, the obsequious waiters, the preening politician entertaining a model at a nearby table all gave her the same feeling of a displaced person that she had suffered for so many years after she came to Dublin. She made herself attend to what Martin was saying. They were celebrating, it seemed, his appointment as principal teacher of the school he had taught in for years. He had always expected to get the job but had said nothing, fearing disappointment. Judy congratulated him, aware that she didn't sound enthusiastic enough – her northern reticence hampered her.

'So now we can get married,' Martin said, surprising her into the retort, 'So what was preventing us all along?' She was dismayed at the tart sound of it but he explained reasonably, 'Don't you know I was afraid I wouldn't be able to keep you in style? You always look so elegant, so expensive. I couldn't bear to think of you with small children spoiling your looks and your clothes and not enough money to buy more. I wanted to have everything beautiful for you – you are such a perfectionist. But now we can manage – don't you think? When will we get married – the summer? I am impatient, Judy.' He smiled at her and she was filled with a ferocious glee that after taking her for granted so long he had now lost her. She was not going to marry him or anybody else but there was no need yet to tell him. The nerves in her fingertips remembered the solidity of the lump.

Her mother had died of cancer. She knew about it from the outside. She had glimpsed the wound where her mother's breasts had been but never brought herself to tend it. She had sat by her mother's bed, bitter at the loss of her warmth, holding her hand but avoiding her painful frightened eyes. As her mother dwindled, her austere husband had become more and more chilly and distant as he efficiently looked after her physical needs. She couldn't imagine Martin doing that for her; he was far too fastidious. She watched his long fingers with the neatly filed shapely nails.

'I just loved you, Martin,' she said. 'I would not have cared about lack of money. We could have been married after your mother died and I would have rejoiced in your children. They would have been half-reared by now and your increase in pay would cope with the extra expense of their education.' She was afraid she was going to cry and he was looking uncomfortable, so she hunted in her bag for the glasses she had never let him see. After polishing them with her handkerchief she put them on and everything around showed up more clearly and more flawed. In his relief he was volubly admiring and then told her all the ins and outs of his appointment.

While he talked she thought of the concentration she had always brought to bear in the past on every word he said. She'd lived on that, imprinted on her mind, until the next time they were together. She'd examined it all for significance or promise. She'd wondered desperately how much of it was real truth and how much just Martin's shade of truth. Tonight none of it mattered. She supposed she was suffering from shock, but she was still aware of the slight distaste she always felt when she watched his lips touch the swirl of cream on the top of his Irish coffee. She had never sampled it herself; she drank her coffee black and unsweetened.

In the carpark outside, a cold east wind blew in from the sea. The lights from the car-ferry showed the waves black and choppy. Martin put his arm for a moment on her stiff shoulders.

'We'll go back to the bungalow,' he said as he started the engine, giving his attention to driving out from the rows of cars.

'Oh no,' she said, 'I must go back to the flat. I'm tired.'

'But we've a lot to discuss.'

'Some other time. I have to think.'

'You're not nervous of me, are you?' he asked, smiling.

She smiled too, but thought to herself that she never had any need for that. When he stopped under the tree outside the gate he put his hand on her arm, but she climbed out hurriedly, warning him of the danger from traffic if he parked there – he had told her of this frequently.

Back in her own room she shivered, stepped out of her high-heeled shoes and put on the kettle for her hot-water bottle. It was a relief to be alone, she realised, such a relief to be rid of Martin. She thought, as she often did, of her father alone, sitting dead in his chair. She hadn't seen him, being in Dublin, but she had been told. He had lived on his own after her mother died, capable, clean, withdrawn. He had let neither his children nor his neighbours have a key to his house, so they had had to break a window to find him. The fire was burnt out, his eyes were closed, his body was cold. 'Wasn't it a terrible lonely way to die?' her sisters said. They looked at her in surprise when she said, 'But he was whole, don't you see. There wasn't a mark on him.'

Maybe the lump was nothing at all. Maybe she would live to a desiccated old age. She had money saved. She'd get a house of her own.

As the kettle came to the boil she looked at the cactus. 'I really should destroy it,' she thought. 'I could empty it into the fireplace without touching the thorns.' She lifted the heavy poker provided, Mrs Robinson had told her, for fear of intruders. She contemplated battering the cactus to pieces on the hearth. 'But it's too late in the night to make such a noise. Far too late,' she told herself, even though a bus raced up the road bringing down a gentle sifting of plaster inside the wall. Someone coming home banged a gate so that it clanged shut and then sprang open again, to swing noisily all night in the wind, keeping Judy company each time she wakened.

A Ghost Story

A Ghost Story

The house was a cause of dissension between them from the first. Fiona said her father would buy them a house for their wedding present, as he had done for her three sisters. He was a builder, of the kind who drove round in a polished Rover and wore gloves while he inspected his sites. He not only had money now, but his people had been rich for generations which was a source of wonder to Fintan. It was one of the things that attracted him to Fiona. She appeared to him as some aureate butterfly that he hoped to pin down. But he was not going to sponge on his father-in-law. He insisted they must buy their own house.

'Don't be ridiculous,' Fiona said. 'All your money will go on paying for the house and mine will go on housekeeping and we'll have nothing to spend. I thought we'd have a lovely life together, but not if you insist on this.'

'We have to pay our way first if I'm to have any self-respect,' Fintan said, surprising himself.

'Such a peasant attitude,' she teased.

'Oh well you can take the man out of the bog but not the bog out of the man,' Fintan quoted his father, a big handsome school-inspector who was given to such dicta.

'I'm not discussing turbary rights,' Fiona laughed, and he laughed back, but the problem remained, holding up their wedding until an agent told him one day that he could sell him a house for twenty-five thousand pounds. It had been on his hands for several years – he just wanted rid of it. He'd settle for twenty-five thousand. It was a modest detached house built in the sixties and never lived in for more than a few months at a time because it was said to be haunted. But since Fintan was a modern young man who wouldn't heed such womanish nonsense he could pick up a bargain. Fintan said he'd have to consult Fiona and the agent raised his eyebrows and turned down the corners of his mouth.

Fiona thought the house was cute in a way but the rooms were smaller and the ceiling lower than anything she'd been used to. Besides, the kitchen was just a small square with a sink unit and the main bedroom had doors across one alcove by way of a built-in wardrobe. Fintan thought she was using these complaints as excuses, that she was really worried about the ghosts. He pointed out that if the house had been old he could have understood ghosts, but since the house the two old ladies were supposed to have lived in had been completely razed and this one built on the site he didn't see how ghosts could have survived. If it would make Fiona any easier in her mind they could get a priest, he was sure, to come and bless the place. Fiona scoffed at him, 'You know I don't go along with all that mumbo-jumbo.'

'I'm never too sure about you,' Fintan said. 'You roll out with your family every Sunday like a dutiful daughter.'

Fintan himself lived in a flat, having been asked by his father to leave home because he wouldn't go to Mass. 'I'm not criticising your religion or the lack of it,' his father had said. 'It is your own affair. And as far as the Almighty is concerned I'm sure you are just one of the flies flattened on the windscreen. But your mother sees things differently and I'm not going to have you worrying her Sunday after Sunday.'

'I can't be dishonest,' Fintan protested. 'I've got to make my own statement. I can't pretend, just to please my mother.'

'There's many a better man than yourself did just that all his life and maybe got to heaven at the heels of the hunt. But if you won't, just take yourself off quietly to a flat of your own. Say it's to leave more room at home for your brothers. But leave her in peace and don't have her saying Rosaries night after night in bed when she thinks I'm asleep.'

'She was always religious. It's not just for me.'

'Until you began troubling her she never said Rosaries when I was in the bed,' his father stated, and Fintan had moved out with no recriminations anywhere.

He found the wedding awkward from that angle – a huge number of guests, a plethora of priests, and Fintan had to explain beforehand that he would not receive Holy Communion. Fiona did, devoutly to all appearances, but during the honeymoon she neglected Mass, not mentioning it at all. It was their economic approach to life that provided a series of surprises for both of them. Even though they earned similar salaries, prices meant entirely different things to each. Fintan looked forward to coming back to his own house where he was sure their lives would blend better.

He had had no objection to presents of carpets and furniture from his rich in-laws, but his tastes were different and he saw no reason to keep quiet about that. Fiona wanted him to accept gifts quietly, whether the suites were too big or the patterns too striking. He complained that he had to live with them and she'd have to adjust herself to smaller rooms. He went round auction rooms and bought small pieces of old furniture. One he had especially loved was a walnut desk with moss-green leather on the writing place, and little drawers with wooden handles all delicately turned and never a nail or a rough edge to be seen. He gave it to Fiona for a present but her offhand acceptance hurt him. He borrowed a spade from a brother-in-law and tackled the front garden. It was stony and grey. A neighbour stopped in passing and advised him that he'd never grow anything in that barren patch unless he got a few loads of topsoil and manure as everyone else had done. 'What is topsoil?' Fintan wondered, but assured the neighbour that he'd see about it and stood the spade in the garage with relief.

When the house was more or less painted and furnished they decided to have a house-warming. They agreed that a brunch party some Sunday would suit and they'd have their own friends, leaving out all the middle-aged people who were at the wedding. On the Friday before the party they got an anonymous letter in the post telling them they ought to know that their house was haunted by the two old ladies knitting. They laughed, passed the letter to each other across the table, relishing it, and argued over who should bring it into work to share the joke there. In the end Fintan took it, with Fiona agreeing to wait until Monday.

The brunch was not really a success. They had thought that the party would begin around noon and end about four in the afternoon, but nobody went home until all the wine had been drunk and by then it was nearly eleven o'clock at night. Fintan enjoyed that, but Fiona was annoyed because things didn't turn out as she had expected. Besides, a close friend of Fintan's, whom she was meeting for the first time, disliked her and took every opportunity to sneer at her cooking, her decorating, her wealth and her father's wealth. Fiona laughed it off so that nobody else felt uncomfortable and to divert them she produced the anonymous letter and handed it around. People started talking about haunted houses they had heard of, at a distance. They all agreed a new house could not possibly be haunted, although somebody said, 'How about the air waves?' One girl had heard her grandfather tell of a cottage in the bog. The man who lived alone there brought in his friend to visit after they left the pub. They drew up their chairs to the fire and a third chair drew up from the far wall on its own accord.

'I see, James, you have company tonight,' the friend said.

'That, John,' said the owner of the house, 'is company that I am seldom without.'

Fiona, watching Fintan listening intently, was resentful that he should seem so detached from her, and when at last the guests took themselves off she attacked him. 'How could you let him insult me all day? You could easily have made him stop. Anyway, I don't know how you could even have liked such an ill-mannered creature.' Fintan shrugged and rubbed his cheek with his hand. Glaring at him, Fiona could feel, as his fingers did, the warm dry skin of his face. She wanted to put her cheek against the broad plane of his forehead. 'You don't love me at all,' she complained, and went into the sitting-room to collect more glasses. Fintan looked, a bit helplessly, at the mess of dirty serving plates on the kitchen table. He was annoyed that Philip hadn't liked Fiona but he hadn't blamed Philip. Fiona was his wife; therefore she should have been in herself pleasing to his friend. It was awkward that they didn't like each other. He supposed they were jealous since they were both attached to him. What, after all, was love? His mother loved him, of course. That was natural. Mothers love their children. And, he assumed, his father loved his mother – all that business of protecting her from worry about him. He didn't feel like protecting Fiona. She was a big girl, clever, rich. It might be the way he felt after making love successfully, but then when she found him inadequate he felt like slitting her throat. She came into the kitchen, clattering glasses. 'We'll have to knock down that wall between those two rooms,' she said. 'I can't bear that little poky room. It gives me claustrophobia.'

Fintan protested. 'We've just painted the whole place white to give you space. We're not going to start knocking down walls. Anyway, it's a supporting wall.'

'Come in and I'll show you what we could do,' she said, putting her two hands on his arm and feeling him tense against her.

'What idiot turned on the television?' she exclaimed when they were at the sitting-room door. The sound had gone wrong. On the screen was an old-fashioned room with a coal fire in a black iron fireplace and an old lady sitting in a rocking chair knitting and talking vigorously, but it was impossible to make out a word she was saying. 'Somebody's been fooling with the buttons,' Fiona said. 'Turn it off.'

'It's not on,' Fintan said exultantly. 'The plug's out.'

She gripped his arm then but he didn't notice; he was concentrating hard on the picture and on the strange light old voice. She was a fine-looking old lady with white straight hair brushed back into a bun at the nape of her neck. She wore little gold-rimmed glasses and a black skirt and blouse with a jet rectangular brooch at the throat. She put down her knitting and took up a hank of wool, spreading it round her knees to wind it into a ball. She had a black shiny apron with a black frill all the way round. The rocking chair moved as she wound the wool. Above the rockers the wooden frame was composed of little carved pillars and the seat was like a deckchair seat, only made from some kind of carpet material. Gaslight came from two globes on curved arms from the wall above the fireplace. The fire itself was only slightly red, not blazing, not reflected in the brass fire irons on the black iron fender.

Opposite the rocking chair was a wing chair and a figure in it practically hidden and silent, perhaps sleeping.

They stood watching, transfixed, until the picture faded. Fiona whispered, 'The two old ladies knitting,' and then they both corrected that, 'But it was a man. In the big chair it was a man.' They were quite sure, although when the picture was there it had been impossible to see. Fiona was trembling. Fintan was nervous but exuberant, wanting to telephone their friends and tell them, unable to stay still. Fiona suggested that they continue clearing up, that maybe it hadn't happened, she didn't really believe it had happened. It was the wine they had drunk during the day. It was late when they went to bed, Fiona reluctantly, as if there was thunder in the air. They lay stiffly on their backs, not touching.

For several nights after that they stayed out of the house until late and hurried to bed without looking into the sitting-room, but everything seemed quiet and gradually, without mentioning it to each other or to anyone else, they pushed it to the back of their minds. Fiona even brought up the idea again of knocking down the wall between the two rooms. Fintan said no. Fiona thought her father could be consulted before they scotched the idea out of hand. Fintan said no, it was his house and nothing at all to do with her father. He had bought a haunted house so as to owe nothing to her father and he wasn't going to backtrack now over a silly notion of hers. 'That wall stays up,' he shouted, thumping against it.

The television screen flickered and bright horizontal lines ran from the bottom to the top. The unintelligible commentary began before the picture settled. This time the woman was on her knees at the rocking chair which had come unstuck and had lurched to the side away from the fire. The little pillars that held the top part of the chair to the rockers were out of their sockets and she was trying to fix them in. When she got one in another hopped out. The man still sat silent in his big solid chair. After a time she began to cry, a childish cry which increased in volume until it was a terrible wail, on and on. 'God,' Fiona breathed, but Fintan gripped her arm and she put her hands over her mouth. Eventually it all faded, the crying persisting for some seconds after the picture went.

'I can't stand this,' Fiona said. 'I can't live here.'

Fintan was too shaken to hear what she said. During the next month they saw the quiet scene several times, so that Fintan said he was growing quite fond of the old lady. Fiona didn't answer him. Then one night the kneeling woman appeared again, and the broken chair and the same crying. Fiona said, 'Do something, can't you. Don't just stand there.' Fintan spread his hands helplessly and she rushed into the kitchen and came back carrying a stool. He grabbed at her arm and said, 'Don't, you can't,' but she whirled the stool at the television set, smashing it through the screen and dealing it blow after blow. Fintan felt outrage at the ugly look on Fiona's face and at the wrong use of the sturdy little pine stool with 'Made in Poland' printed in black under the seat. When she turned triumphantly to him, still brandishing the stool, he felt frightened for a moment that she meant to attack him. Instead she said, 'There! That's settled it. How long would you have stood there before you realised some action was called for? The active sex! God Almighty!'

'The set was rented. How are we going to pay the company?' Fintan said.

'Money again. I'll pay if you're so upset.'

'You just may. You broke it.' He put the broken set out with the dustbin the following Friday and they had no more television and no more ghostly films.

Fiona was careful to be gentle, having frightened herself with her demonstration of violence. She acquiesced in whatever Fintan wanted, even when he suggested that it would be better if they went out separately now and again to avoid feeling suffocated. They didn't talk about their experiences, but as the weeks went by they relaxed and settled amicably enough together. Then they were invited to a party given by Fintan's friend Philip. Fiona said she wouldn't go; Fintan could make what excuse he liked but she would spend the evening in comfort at home in her parents' house. They wanted her to stay the night in her own old room, all aired and beautiful with its white carpet and mirrored wardrobes and old mahogany bed. They didn't like her driving home to an empty house, probably cold. Fiona laughed, said she did it quite often, and drove off before they persuaded her otherwise. The house *was* cold. It looked cramped and ordinary, just cheap. The bed hadn't softened yet into any degree of cosiness, and she lay reading for an hour before trying to sleep. A full moon shone in on her face when she turned to the window, so she curled up with her back to it. She was restless, missing Fintan, and she told herself resentfully that she'd probably be just asleep when he would come in and waken her. Then she heard the childish crying downstairs and listened in horror until it reached a crescendo of that frightful wailing. She started to cry herself, 'God, God,' huddling under the quilt. As soon as the noise downstairs died away she got up and dressed, gabbling to herself, grabbed her bag and car keys and drove back to her parents' house. Fintan, coming back at four o'clock and seeing the empty tossed bed, felt only relief that he wouldn't have to justify the lateness of the hour or the fact that he was not sober.

Fiona insisted that the house be sold and every stick of furniture in it. She had no wish to break up their marriage. She would live with him in a flat or wherever he liked, but not with anything out of that house. In the meantime she stayed with her parents and Fintan was lucky enough to get the loan of a flat from a friend who was in America on a training course. Selling the furniture they had got from her family gave him no trouble and he forced himself to part with the pieces he had bought, but not with the walnut desk. He told Fiona it was hers, but she exclaimed in horror that she couldn't even look at its little carved pillars and knobs without seeing the rocking chair, that she'd never live in any house it stood in. He brought it to the flat and polished it lovingly.

They met for lunch or parties or concerts. They were still married, just temporarily without living quarters, only celibate for the moment. When a possibility came up of a job in Saudi Arabia he asked her would she come if he got it and she, tired of the ambiguity of her position, agreed, providing he brought nothing pertaining to the house. He called to explain his plans to his parents and found his father alone.

'There aren't any ghosts in the desert,' Fintan laughed.

'What?' his father said. 'With all those mutilations and executions? You amaze me.'

Fintan mentioned his attachment to the desk.

'Give it to your mother,' he was told.

Fintan laughed. 'What on earth would she want with it?'

'She is not illiterate, you know,' his father retorted, and Fintan hurried to apologise that he had not meant to imply that.

'She will care for it because you gave it to her. God knows none of you have given her much, with all your fine jobs.'

'You didn't give her much yourself,' Fintan said, rattled. 'Nothing but the daily paper when you have done with it.'

His father tapped him on the shoulder. 'Your mother and I understand each other. Don't take it on yourself to worry about us.'

'Such arrogance,' Fintan thought, but he took his father's

advice about the desk and was rewarded by his mother's obvious delight. He even managed to sell the house at a small profit to an American who was interested in ghosts.

'You don't realise how very lucky you are,' his mother-in-law told him one day when he called for Fiona before she was ready. She was an elegant woman, partly due to expensive clothes and hair, partly to her very slim figure. He found himself hoping that Fiona would fine down eventually and look like her.

'You have both been given a new chance,' she went on. 'One fright does nobody any harm and you have lost nothing at all. You must have had somebody's prayers,' she finished with an ironic lift to one eyebrow.

'You don't like me,' he said. 'You never thought me good enough for Fiona. Just because I'm not rich.'

'My dear Fintan, there are none of us as rich as people think. Fiona has had a good salary up to now – she didn't need a rich husband. But you are not a kind person. I always wished for my daughters that they would marry kind men. Kindness lasts even if the couple are no longer in love.' Fintan smiled that she should use such a term, and she accused him, 'You are not kind to Fiona.'

'She is not always kind to me,' Fintan answered back childishly. 'Her voice has a very unkind edge to it at times.' His mother-in-law shrugged, and when Fiona came into the room he glared at her so that the happy look on her face slid away. Later on in the evening she asked if it was worthwhile her going out to Saudi Arabia with him at all if he didn't really want her. He said, 'Oh please do, Fiona. I couldn't bear it if you didn't.'

One evening before they left he paid a visit to the house. He had already given up the keys but the American had said it wasn't sensible to move in before the fall. The house didn't look a bit sinister, just slightly pathetic, even though all their curtains had been sold in the deal and still hung at the windows but a little stiffly because no one had touched them for weeks. Fintan regretted the loss of the house, the loss of his status as a citizen and resident with responsibilities in the community. He would even have tackled the garden, he thought, standing and looking at the stony soil with starving ragwort and a couple of frail poppies as its crop. The limestone rock was only two feet down, a neighbour had said, but on this patch it seemed to be breaking through. At least in the desert the sand would cover the bones. He didn't really mind the poor old ghosts. He could have lived with them, even though the crying was hard to take. But then all crying was hard to take. He thought of Fiona and the brightness gone so rapidly from their life. The sadness shook him so that his legs trembled and wouldn't move out of the garden. Sweat broke out on his neck and head even though it was a cool evening for early September with a bank of mist along the foot of the mountains. He reached out to steady himself and held on to the iron railing he'd painted black after they moved in. The spasm passed and he let go, but when he saw a black stain on the palm of his hand he scrubbed at it in panic. Once he had shut himself into the security of his car he wondered had Fiona felt like this during previous emanations while he didn't, and if so was she in this way and, who knows, perhaps in other ways a protection to him. He could manage to be kind, he was sure, if he practised, if that would please her and keep her with him, especially in a strange country with no friends and no position other than as his wife. The street lamp glowed red, suggesting dusk, and he switched on his own lights and drove away from the house, only very slightly shaken now, to meet Fiona in town.

Inheritance

Inheritance

The last day of Joan's last carefree holiday was hot and overcast. Looking for a cool place, she wandered across the fields among her father's sleek cattle to the old water-course that was one boundary of his farm. Her father used to bring her there for a walk on Sunday evenings when she was a little girl, the last of the family, holding her hand in his that even then was gnarled. He had pointed out to her the danger of its depth if she should fall in, not only in the steadily flowing water, but in the perpendicular walls of parallel slabs of dark-grey lime-stone with only the odd branch of bramble trailing down from field level. He had told her it had been cut out and the walls built in famine times. Reaching over, with his stick he had pointed out to her the even solidity of the building, the carefully matched stones. 'Think of those poor half-starved divils working at that to bring home at the end of the day a fistful of yellow-meal to the pot-bellied children, too hungry to cry.'

She didn't think of them, either then or later, but he had said the words so often they stuck in her mind like a prayer or a nursery rhyme. The water was strictly confined. It had none of the sparkle and dash of a natural river, but in the greatest droughts, her father said, it was always there to be relied upon. It was no cooler there that day than anywhere else, so Joan walked back along the land that a local flying club had leased for an airstrip.

The house was dark and the kitchen heat smelled of the plum jam her mother was stirring in her big brass preserving pan on the cooker. Wasps zoomed in the open door and buzzed, trapped, against the windows that were stuck with successive coats of paint and couldn't be opened. Her mother wiped the sweat from under her chin with the back of her hand and smiled at her. Joan went upstairs to begin her packing for an early train the next day back to Dublin and her good job in the civil service. When she came down later, the jam was in neatly covered jars on a tray on the table, the kitchen was cleared and her mother was asleep in one of the armchairs, her hands in her lap, her head dropped sideways. Joan stood looking at her and thought, 'My mother is old.'

A few weeks later, when the satisfaction of her job and the security of her own flat had put all thought of her parents out of her head, her brother called to see her. He was on his way back to London, having spent his holiday on the farm.

'They're getting old,' he warned Joan. 'If I were you I'd get myself tied up somehow like the rest of us or they'll be expecting you to go back home and nurse them into their graves.'

Joan was horrified. 'They wouldn't expect me to give up my job!'

'I'm only warning you,' he said, and went off to catch his plane.

Joan remembered going to town as a little girl hand in hand with her mother and meeting other countrywomen who said, 'And is this the little housekeeper?' before going on to discuss ailments, operations and hospitals.

Most of her contemporaries were married, but she had no

great difficulty in finding Ian Gillespie. His flatmate had just left to get married himself, and he was on his own with no one to share the rent. He cast nervous glances at Joan when they bumped into each other at parties. He had little to say for himself but Joan didn't suppose that mattered, nor that he looked undistinguished. She was well aware of her own angular plainness. He worked in insurance and earned rather less than she did, but in a way that was satisfactory.

They were married in Dublin to save her parents the trouble of a big reception. They bought an expensive house. Their combined salaries enabled them to make large mortgage repayments, to furnish the house as they wished and left them plenty for entertainment. They had their friends in to admire everything and to eat curry and drink wine. A nun in Joan's school had told the senior girls that the primary object of marriage was not the procreation of children, as some taught, but that both partners should lead each other to God. So Joan had no scruples about taking the contraceptive pill, and she led Ian to mini-weekends in holiday hotels, to rent an Irish cottage with two other couples in Ballyvaughan, to an October fortnight in Rhodes.

Ian was not an ardent lover. Joan had to admit to herself that she was generally disappointed. She wondered were they perhaps rushing around too much, but the thought of sitting in the armchairs, facing each other across the coal-effect fire, daunted her. Some nights, dropping asleep, she was too tired to remember if she'd taken her pill or not.

One day, about a year after the wedding, she read down the first paper of a file in her office and realised she hadn't taken in a word of it. She re-read it, concentrating, and wondered what was the matter with her. Usually her mind was sharp. She went home to the country to rest without Ian for a long weekend. She yawned over breakfast in her own cool bed, sat dozing in a sunny corner of her mother's garden and swallowed iron tablets.

'Is it not just nature?' asked her mother.

'What do you mean – nature?' Joan demanded.

'She means are you expecting a baby,' her older sister, who had six children, explained.

'But how could I be?'

'It's usual enough,' her mother said drily, 'unless there's something wrong with Ian.'

The two older women laughed together, to Joan's disgust.

A week later, when the doctor's wife on the telephone assured her brightly that the pregnancy test was positive, she said nothing at all. In the car that evening going home with Ian she sat silent, hating him. When she went into the house she flung open all the windows. He shivered and she turned on him. 'The house smells,' she said. After their meal she took her coffee over to an armchair and sat with her forehead down on her knees.

'Is there anything wrong?' he asked. 'Have I done anything wrong?'

She sat up and looked at him, slight, anxious – his small head, small nose, small mouth. 'I'm pregnant,' she said, and watched what she described to herself as an oafish grin spread over his face. When his pleasure faded he said, 'Oh.'

She didn't hate him all during her pregnancy. She argued herself into a more sensible frame of mind regarding him. She gradually became aware that instead of the old nervousness in his eyes he was looking at her with love. She felt it an added burden, but it deflected her hatred to the predatory poltergeist inside her. She studied the pictures in a book she had bought on childbirth. She concentrated on the two-month foetus – thin arms and legs with stubby hands and feet, pointed bottom, humpy head and an open-eyed malevolent grin. She would pay no attention to its kicks and pummellings. She didn't mention her pregnancy to anyone until it was obvious. She wouldn't discuss it with Ian.

As the months went by her feet swelled, her hands swelled, her face became red and shiny like the big stout countrywomen at home. She hated the sight of herself. Her former brisk efficiency at work deserted her and she was slow and unsure. There was a swing door into her office building. She had a fear that she would stick in it one day and have to be rescued ignominiously. Sometimes bursts of silvery balls like mercury exploded in front of her eyes. On one visit to her doctor she pointed out her flushed face and made one of her rare jokes, 'I seem to be having my first baby and the menopause at the same time.' He laughed politely, but from practice in the civil service in discerning middle-aged men's expressions she knew from the movement of the lines on his forehead that he was not amused. He told her to rest. He mentioned the possibility of total bed rest if she wanted to be sure of carrying her baby full-term.

'Maybe it'll die,' she thought grimly as she walked back to the office.

'Maybe I'll die,' she thought as she dressed to go out with Ian to supper in a friend's house. She sat down on the edge of her bed. She heard Ian in the bathroom shaving, brushing his teeth, whistling as he dried himself. She shrugged and forced her feet into her shoes.

Her friends were kind to her, seeing that she had the most comfortable chair and the place of honour. They were interested and wanted to talk about the baby. Ian was watching her solicitously. 'I believe there's some kind of frog,' she said loudly and clearly, and the room fell silent, 'and when the eggs are at an early stage the female puts them into the male's mouth and he swallows them and incubates them until they are ready to be born, when they come out of his mouth live little struggling frogs hopping and squatting.' Some of the women gave little screams. One said yes she'd seen it on television. Ian choked on his chilli con carne.

Later in bed he didn't kiss her goodnight but turned his back on her straight away. When at last she settled herself fairly comfortably and dropped asleep, she dreamed that she was up to her arms in the watercourse and although her head was above water she couldn't breathe with the compression of her chest. She woke gasping for breath and sat up in a panic. The breathlessness did not go away, so she went into the bathroom for an aspirin and found she could not take a drink without a frightening feeling of suffocation. When Ian staggered out sleepily after her to see what was wrong, she flung herself at him as she had never done before and put her arms around his neck, crying, 'Oh Ian, you'll have to help me. I can't manage. I can't. I can't.' He was alarmed at first, but then reassuring, and brought extra pillows to prop her up in bed the way he said his mother slept most of her life.

She had to stop work. She spent her days in bed lying half awake. The house was dulled with dust. Ian did the shopping cheerfully but there were gaps in necessities. The food was a fiasco. They moved her into hospital where everybody spoke to her gently as if a thoughtless breath would make her fall apart. She kept her childbirth book beside the bed and from it practised her relaxation and breathing for the birth. The book frequently fell open at a picture of a fat contented baby, arms folded and legs curled up. Sometimes, when she felt no movement inside her for several days, she found anxiety niggling at her. She knew by the doctor's carefully arranged cheerful smile that he was worried, and gradually it became her duty to produce a healthy baby just as it had earlier been her duty and satisfaction to do her job well. She prided herself on being reliable.

When labour began the nurses suggested that Ian stay with her and he sat on the edge of his chair looking terrified. She had to keep rousing herself to reassure him, so after a while she sent him away. 'You do know I love you,' he said before he went, but she hardly heard him. She conducted herself perfectly. They told her she was wonderful, and after her son was born they beamed at her so happily she would have smiled too, if she had been able to keep her eyes open. She could hear him crying.

She had never held a baby in her arms. When her sisters' and brothers' children were born she had wondered at her mother's excitement. She hadn't liked being left to fend for herself when her mother rushed off to help out with new grandchildren. She had taken little interest in them. She was godmother to none. Now she held her own son diffidently. When the nurse gave her a feeding bottle half-full, she didn't know how to hold it, or him, or how to get it into his mouth. In her awkwardness the teat brushed against his cheek and he seized on it, sucking strongly. Joan felt very competent as she saw the bottle empty. A nurse put her head around the door. 'I'll be back in a minute to help you,' she said, and Joan sat waiting until her stiff arms had to relax round the sleeping little body. Eventually the nurse tucked him into his glass cot and Joan found herself smiling looking at him, so compact, so self-contained, like an expensive pocket calculator. She told herself that it was objective admiration for a piece of good design, but when some days later he was pushed in crying with hunger and no bottle arrived for ten minutes she was shaking with distress and anger. She carried him over to the window and tried to distract him. 'Look up there,' she told him. 'That's the sky.' He was quiet for a moment and the high dark-grey clouds were the same colour as his eyes. She was always relieved when he was taken away to the nursery. She did not like this onslaught on her feelings. Nevertheless she knew before she left the hospital that she was going to rear the baby herself.

Some weeks later Ian asked her when she was supposed to take up her job again since she had been off so long before the birth. 'I'm not going back,' she said. 'I have to stay at home and look after the baby. There isn't anybody else to do it.'

'We could get somebody,' Ian said. 'Other people do.'

'Other people are not going to rear my child,' Joan said flatly.

'You're not an expert,' Ian ventured. 'You really know nothing about rearing children.'

'I can learn, and I'll never be careless. And he's my child and I intend to rear him myself.'

'We'll have to leave this house then, and get a cheaper one. My pay won't run to much.'

'Well then, we'll leave this house. It's not important where we live.'

He gave up, not knowing where to turn.

Her mother arrived on her ritual visit. She sat with her grandson on her knee. 'It's a pity I'm so old,' she said in a matter-of-fact voice. 'I could have looked after him for you to let you back to work. You don't want a stranger with him while he's so young.'

'I'm not going back to work,' Joan said. 'I'm staying at home to rear him myself.' At the same time she felt sudden resentment that her mother was so old, no use at all to a growing boy in a year or two. He'd need grandparents to give him a solid base, and here they were already in their seventies. Ian's parents she dismissed as weightless, a wisp of a man and a woman propped up with pillows – people of no consequence.

'What will you do for money?' her mother asked. 'Ian doesn't earn that much.'

'We'll have to sell the house and get a smaller one,' Joan said. 'It's a pity because there's a good sunny garden here that would do very well for putting the pram in and for a toddler to play in. But it can't be helped. It takes my salary to pay off the mortgage.'

'I'll get the money for you to pay off the house,' her mother said firmly.

Joan gaped at her. 'Where would you get the money?'

'I'll get it from your father.'

'How would he have it?'

'He has a lot put by. And if need be we can sell a few acres. We could buy your house ten times over with the price of land nowadays. We're getting too old to need it all now. These last years we've done well, and I'd rather you'd get it than the income tax.'

'He won't think that way.'

'He'll do anything I ask him.'

Joan looked at her mother in surprise, remembering her hard work and poor appearance all down the years, the 'good' navy coat, hat and shoes that had seen her into town and to Sunday Mass for as long as Joan could look back. 'You mustn't have asked him for much,' she said.

'I never asked him for anything for myself so that he could never refuse what I asked for my children.'

'His too.'

Her mother laughed. 'Oh, his too, but it's not the same for them at all. They get off very easily. I always suspected that, but I knew it for certain when you were six. You had a kidney infection and the stupid doctor didn't diagnose it for nearly a fortnight. You were fading away, a pale thin miserable child looking like one the fairies had left. Your father had gone into town on fair day and when he came home in the evening I met him at the door, wringing my hands and my heart knocking with fear for you, and I said, "Robert, I think she's worse today. She couldn't even step out of the bath." And he said, "Who? Who's worse?" and he couldn't think for a minute or two what I was talking about. If it had been a cow and a calf he'd have been worrying all day. They have their own cares and crosses, I have no doubt,' her mother finished, 'but the rearing of children doesn't count for much with them.' She undid the baby's nappy to let him kick freely on her lap. She smiled, watching him. 'Isn't he a grand little man.'

After a while she said, 'So you're giving up your job. I always had a wish to have one daughter independent, not beholden to any man for money. The other three are settled happily, well off and not a penny to call their own. I was so proud of you with your degree and your fine job and your own pay. I used to think of you able to take a train or plane off some place without having to make out a case to get the fare.'

That night in bed Joan was anxious waiting for the baby to fall asleep. She was aware of the restlessness of her mother in the strange bed in the next room, but it was the creaking of the Moses basket beside her that kept her awake. Her sister had offered her the loan of it and she hadn't cared enough beforehand to refuse. Now she thought if she had her own money she'd have gone out straight away and bought a quieter cot. The baby himself fought every night either to get to sleep or to stay awake, Joan wasn't sure which. He twisted and kicked, arched his back, grunted and wrestled to get his thumb into his mouth. Every now and again he gave a frustrated howl. Joan agonised with him, sweat trickling down her body. Would this oppression, this anxiety, stay with her all his life? she wondered. Was this perhaps what love was? What experience had she of love? She remembered the comfort of her mother's hug when she came home from town and put her parcels on the kitchen table and the house felt right again. She remembered the warm dryness of her father's hand round hers, going for Sunday walks. Even Ian, perhaps a little bit she had loved, coming into the house after a pleasant evening and admiring the sage-green walls and moss-green carpet of the hall and stairs. These had made her feel safe, soft, secure. In no way were they akin to what she felt for the baby. She could understand how some women murdered their babies to save themselves from the possibility of the child's sickness or accident, from bullies and gangs, from vindictive teachers and examinations. She groaned, thinking of the future, and Ian jumped up out of his sleep. 'What is it, Joan? What's the matter? What's wrong?' She quelled him. 'Oh, nothing you would know about. What does it matter to you?' He pleaded, 'Ah Joan, you shouldn't be like that,' but he lay down again and seemed to be asleep. 'No, indeed I shouldn't,' she thought to herself. After all, he had to support them in a way he'd never bargained for. Also, in time, the baby would need brothers and sisters. She patted his back kindly and then cautiously put her arm around him. He reached up and held her hand tightly in his. It was not very comfortable and kept her awake.

The baby at last slept soundly. The light from street lamps on the road behind shone on the bedroom wall, barred by the parallel slats of the open blinds. The wind in an old tree in the garden made shadows wave across the reflection. When Joan's eyes closed she was back on the bank of the watercourse, looking down the straight stretch of its hard-earned monotonous flow.

The Bricks Are
Fallen Down

The Bricks Are Fallen Down

'Couldn't you give up this notion even now and come home?' Donal said.

Sheila, hurrying along the platform, looked at her husband impatiently. 'With my train ticket bought and paid for? Don't be silly. You know I have to go. I've promised. And I'll be back safe and sound by nine o'clock tonight. Don't forget to meet me.' She tried to make him smile.

'I can't see why you have to go – not after that letter. Some man you knew years ago, that I never even heard about, rings up out of the blue and you have to rush off to Belfast to see him. I don't know why you didn't tell him you're married now and that's that.'

'Am I not allowed to have any friends now? I'm married so I mustn't go to visit any other man even though he's injured and can't go out. Talk about the Ayatollah!'

'It's not that, Sheila. Sure I didn't mind at all until the letter came.'

'An anonymous threatening letter is not going to make me change my plans. I wouldn't please them, whoever it is.'

'They said in the garda station you shouldn't go to Belfast for fear it might mean something.'

'You said they said that. You put words into their mouths. Anyway, I'm here. I'm going. I don't want to fight with you. There's no sense in waiting until the train goes. The children will be wondering what's keeping you. You don't want to leave them too long next door on a Sunday.'

'The children! The children! That's all you care about.'

She didn't contradict him. She didn't look at him because sometimes when she argued he looked pathetic, sometimes he glared at her with what would have passed for hatred. So she peered in through the carriage window and since the train was practically empty she stopped at the nearest door and put her hand on his arm. 'Bye bye, love. Don't wait. I'll see you this evening.'

'Goodbye, Sheila.' He was stiff, courteous, and he went quickly down the platform with an exaggerated jauntiness in his step.

Sheila arranged herself in a corner seat with the Sunday papers he had bought on the table in front of her. She couldn't read because of her desolation at being left suddenly alone away from home. When Donal went and she stayed it didn't ruffle her, but on the odd occasion that she had to venture any distance without him or the children she felt like a child who howls when his mother leaves. She never told him of this. Nor did she tell him when he put into words a thought that had just come into her head. She had not worked out why she should keep him at that distance.

She had shown him the letter straight away, though, when it came in the post earlier in the week. It said:

Mrs Ryan,

We know why you left Belfast. You cannot hide from us.

THE BRICKS ARE FALLEN DOWN

We can pick you out any time we like in Dublin but stay out of Belfast. If you go there you're a dead woman.

The Watchers

The paper was ordinary. It was posted in Dublin the previous day. The writing was clear and definite. When Donal looked up from it, appalled, she shook her head, indicating the three children at the breakfast table. When she went to the door to see him off to work, she said, 'Bring it to the guards.'

'The guards!' he exclaimed. 'But you don't want them thinking you are mixed up in anything!'

'Well I'm not, as they'll soon find out if they make enquiries. It's the only thing to do. People shouldn't get away with the like of that.'

The guards, reported Donal, thought it was nasty but not dangerous. If the Ryans could think who had written it they had ways of frightening such people but without a suspect they could do nothing. When Donal mentioned the Belfast trip she proposed making they said, 'Ah maybe put it off, just to be on the safe side. A woman is always safer in her own home when this kind of nastiness is about.' Donal thought she was unreasonable to refuse their advice.

She didn't see that she had any option. She had loved Paul Taylor before she met Donal, so when his mother on the telephone asked her to come and visit him she had said yes with her head spinning and her mouth dry. She was not going back on her word. She wasn't sure if she wanted to see him, but that didn't matter. She had heard some time before that he was injured in a bomb blast but not seriously. His mother told her that he couldn't leave the house and that he was

47

anxious to see her. 'I suppose he wants to talk about the old times,' his mother suggested.

Sheila remembered the 'old times' quite clearly. She remembered how beautiful he was with his skin tanned from the Middle East and his long elegant hands and legs and his clothes carefully chosen to match his car. She remembered worshipping him, amazed that he should have taken any notice of her, jubilant that he seemed to love her. She remembered the shock she felt when he asked her to come with him to London for a week or even a weekend. 'What would be the sense?' she'd asked, because she had thought they would naturally progress towards marriage.

'No sense,' he'd said, 'just a celebration. You want me. I want you. Belfast is a bit sordid. You'd enjoy London with me to show you around.' Seeing her outwardly refuse, he was annoyed. He jibed at her puritanism, told her she had not the right attitude to her Catholic faith. Real European Latin Catholics were full of love of life, joy in God's creation. She belonged to this grim northern sect which bore no resemblance to life envisaged by Christ in the Holy Land. He knew all those places well. He knew the climate. He knew the passion of those people, so different from her virginal piety. Did she not realise it was really a sublimation of her love of him?

'What would you do if I got pregnant?' she asked him to stop his tongue hurting her.

He had laughed and assured her that that kind of thing did not happen in real life. 'It's not so easy at all to start a baby you know.'

Sitting in the railway carriage Sheila smiled, remembering for the hundredth time that statement. She and Donal had no such difficulty. The train had left the darkness of the station and Sheila saw people coming out of Mass, exchanging greetings, buying papers, taking children by the hand – a sunny summer Sunday in the south. She passed the carefully created green lawns and coloured flowerbed of a park built on land reclaimed by dumping city refuse in the sea and further on the still-exposed piles of garbage where seagulls gyrated squalling into the blue sky and dived scavenging into the tips. Her first baby was born within twelve months of the wedding, the second a year later: two little girls, intact, self-reliant, impervious to the rest of the world, attached to each other, two little smooth fawn heads so often together. Two years later Malachy had been born. Now he was nearly three and they were very careful because everybody agreed that Sheila needed a rest and Malachy was a very demanding, excitable, demonstrative child. Sheila sighed.

She tried to read her papers, telling herself she should be enjoying the peace and quiet, but excitement took hold of her again, making the printed stories meaningless. Since the phone call from Paul's mother in Belfast, recollection of her time with him frequently pushed away Donal and the children so that she didn't hear when they spoke to her, only saw open mouths and moving faces. She had to keep reminding herself that Paul's glamour had come to nothing in the long run, that it was Donal she'd married, it was Donal she loved. It didn't matter that his exuberance had been impoverished by his responsibilities. It was enough that he valued her as she was. He didn't tell her, as Paul had constantly done, that she'd be a marvellous person if only she'd do a dozen things that would make her entirely different. Her life lay in a semi-detached house in Dublin, not a flat in London or at best a bungalow in Bahrain.

'Self-preservation, girls, is the strongest human instinct,' the religion teacher in school had repeatedly told them. The romantic teenagers in her class were indignant, but Sheila found it to be true. She knew it when she refused to go to

London or have any adventures other than marriage, and she was ashamed. She felt it to be despicable and herself alien in a man's world, fit only for her mother's house or the houses of her close friends where they gathered in turn because the dangers in Belfast meant there was no social life in town or across the town. Then Donal was sent by his firm in Dublin to work for three months in their Belfast office where Sheila was. He was lost. At first he couldn't understand what people said and when he got used to that he couldn't understand why they said it. One morning during the coffee break a man in the office who was 'saved' pointed his finger at him and said, 'I'd have you know there is only one intermediary between God and man.' Donal managed to say, 'Yes, sure, sure. I'm sure you're right.' When the man had gone and Sheila was washing the cups, he said to her, 'God, Sheila, is he mad or what? What is he talking about? And my landlady's as bad, only the other way. She swears I'm in the IRA sent up from Dublin and she won't charge me a proper rent – only about half what I should be paying. And when I swear to her I'm in nothing, only sent up by a bloody accountancy firm, she says, "Ah we know you have to say that!" If I sit in her house at night she tells me nobody has called and no messages have been left for me, and if I get a letter from my mother in Tipperary she gets all excited at the Republican stamp and dusts round me. And if I go out I get into the wrong street or I ask for the *Irish Press* in the wrong shop or I'm told by some tight-mouthed old one, "We don't take no foreign money here." Now there's that nut in there shaping up to shoot me.'

Sheila reassured him, 'Mr Scott won't shoot you or anyone else. He is only interested in your soul.'

Sheila had found him digs in her own quiet mixed area in an old three-storey house owned by two sisters on pension who smoked all day and at night drank hot whiskeys while listening to the RUC on their transistor. She brought him home often or to her friends' houses for the parties they cooked up. Donal moved easily in their company, using names more often than Sheila's acquaintances did, obviously thinking nothing of a hand on a shoulder or on an arm. Her mother treated him casually even though he complimented her on her cooking and brought her flowers. She had been taken in by Paul's charm, and expected him as a son-in-law.

Donal was with them at the table when a bomb went off at the grocer's shop at the corner. Sheila's mother blessed herself, as she did during thunderstorms, and said, 'Jesus, Mary and Joseph.' Loose plaster fell in a corner from the ceiling and soot plonked down the chimney and billowed black all over the room. Sheila found herself on her knees with her hands clasped, and Donal was helping her up, asking over and over, 'Are you all right, Sheila? Are you all right?'

'Another blow for Irish freedom,' her father said sarcastically. 'I'll just go out and see what's happened.'

'I'll run over and have a word with Miss Ogle. She's house-proud – she won't take kindly to this,' her mother said. 'I can leave you, Sheila, to clear up here.'

So they brushed and washed, but in the middle of it Donal said, 'Sheila, I'm going back to Dublin in a fortnight. I can't bear to think of leaving you in this hellish place. Would you think of coming to Dublin with me?'

'What do you mean?' Sheila asked carefully, wondering was this a new gimmick, but when he asked her clearly to marry him she said yes with surprise and joy.

The train slowed down as it came to the border where the line was most frequently bombed. All that remained of Goraghwood station was a wall, part scarred brick, part broken bathroom-style tiles. The name had featured in all the stories her mother's generation had told of trips to Dublin during the

war, when violent death was a large and impersonal phenom-
enon, not a bullet in a back entry or a body in a ditch. The
little roads and patchy fields of that hilly country were deserted.

Her mother had tried to dissuade her from the engagement;
a tiff with Paul could soon be made up, she was trying to
escape from Belfast, she didn't know Donal well enough.
When she saw they were determined she told people, 'He's an
accountant in Dublin,' but if Sheila or Donal were there they
insisted on the truth, that he was not really an accountant
since he had not sat for all the examinations. He hadn't
bothered. As their expenses went up and the value of his salary
went down, he began to lament his early laziness and to
apologise to her that he'd never be rich. Sheila had to stop
herself hankering for a new coat or boots. She stopped
window-shopping because it worried him. Her mother gave
the children presents of clothes and conspired with Sheila to
keep them lovely. The train fare today was a cause of guilt to
her. She'd had to ask Donal for it and, though he'd given it
as he always gave her what she asked for, he'd counted the
notes left in his wallet with his lips pursed. Sheila often thought
how happy she would be if she had just a little money of her
own, but then she upbraided herself for being mercenary and
proud.

'How will I look to Paul?' she thought. She'd had her coat
cleaned in a one-day cleaner's but it didn't look like new; it
looked like an old coat that had been cleaned. She'd made her
dress herself on a second-hand sewing-machine she'd bought
and it did nothing for her. A photographer taking pictures of
the children once told her how he'd frequently wondered at
husbands who, seeing photographs of their undistinguished
wives, said, 'Isn't she beautiful? You must admit it – isn't she
really beautiful?' Paul would not see her like that. She wished
she'd told his mother on the phone that she couldn't get away.

She was a fool to waste her time and Donal's money setting herself up to be jeered at. She was to be met by a girl in a yellow Volkswagen which would be in the station yard. Suppose she just hurried out of the station and got a bus to her old home and knocked on the door. Her mother would come out and lift up her hands in delight and kiss her and call to her father, 'Look who's here. Look who we have.' He would come out of the kitchen still holding his newspaper and say, 'What's up? Is there anything wrong?' Her mother would give him a little push and say, 'Of course not. Sure there isn't, Sheila?' She smiled, thinking of them.

Time was when she could have pushed the front door open, but not any more. It was locked and bolted like everyone else's since the sectarian murders. One day her mother, busy making crab-apple jelly in the kitchen, had been startled by a loud knocking at the yard door. She'd been afraid to open it and had screamed when she saw two blackened hands appearing over the top of the yard wall. Through her screams she'd heard at last a man's voice calling, 'It's the coal, Mrs, only the coal!' She'd drawn the bolt on the yard door and they had looked at each other shakily and apologised. Because they were both so upset she insisted on bringing him in for a cup of tea in spite of coal marks on her floor and chair. She generously spread the apple jelly on his bread and, not yet set, it dribbled on his black hands which he licked, assuring her, 'Grand jelly, Mrs. I'm all right now, Mrs, but it's not right to have us all so frightened. It's not right and no good will come of it.'

From her train window Sheila could see the clear dark line of the Belfast hills against a grey sky, ending in the Cave Hill and MacArt's Fort, jutting basalt. There, early settlers had watched the whole area for invaders but, Sheila wondered, what kind of people stayed in the fort and what kind went off

53

into the country hoping for a way to live normally. As a child on Sunday walks she had been shown where the losers in any fight were hurled off the cliff. She had imagined desperate fingers clinging to the black rock-face. 'We haven't advanced much,' Sheila thought, and checked in her mirror that she was as presentable as she could be.

The new station was a dismal place and Sheila was never too sure where it was geographically. The carpark was nearly empty so the yellow car was easily seen. Sheila picked her way round big pools from early rain. The girl in the driver's seat reached over to open the car door for her, smiling stiffly. 'You must be Sheila?' Sheila judged her to be in her late twenties, beautifully made-up. 'Do you live near Paul?' she asked as the car was capably eased over ramps. She wondered what was the girl's connection with him.

'Oh no, indeed I don't. I've known him for years. I knew him before he was hurt. I wouldn't think much of myself if I left him to himself now.'

Sheila felt uncomfortable, needing to explain that she'd been married for seven years and hadn't seen Paul for some time before that. They drove in an awkward silence through the empty city centre until they reached a terrace with bricked windows and slates slithering off the roofs. A picture of flowers had been painted on the end wall but a hole had been battered through it. In the middle of the row the Volkswagen pulled up and the girl said, 'There you are,' nodding towards an occupied house. The paint was fresh, the door brasses shining, buff-coloured blinds with scalloped edges hung well down with red geraniums in pots filling the space beneath. Sheila hesitated but the girl said, 'Paul lives with his mother now. That's her house. I'll call back for you in good time for the train.' Sheila protested that it was unnecessary but the girl waved and drove away and Sheila was left at the doorstep. On the other side of the street was a waste patch, gritty, uneven, littered with broken bricks. A shored-up gable wall marked the beginning of another row of deserted houses. Sheila had to stop a feeling of fear – just with the letter and the desolation – but the house door opened behind her and the strong Belfast accent she had heard on the phone bade her come in.

'Why didn't Eithne bring you in? She's got a key to the house so that she can come in and out, if I'm away a message or something, without disturbing Paul. How are you, Sheila? I never met you. Time was I wouldn't be let meet Paul's friends but pride takes a fall. Isn't that right, Paul?' she said, conducting Sheila into a sitting-room where even in the dim light Sheila could see everything was spotless and neat. Paul lay in an armchair, his long legs straight out, his head against a lace-edged linen chairback. He wore big dark glasses so that Sheila could not see if he were awake or asleep, and he didn't move.

'Come on,' his mother said, 'don't be playing at being dead. I'm telling Sheila here that your mother is good enough for you now. Changed times, Sheila! I suppose you saw the grand flat he used to have on the Malone Road? Eithne knew her way round it all right but I never saw it until I had to get his things out when he told me in the hospital he was going to live here. I never was invited. I never even knew was he in the country or out of it. I was always expecting to be told he was married without letting on to me. But here he is now. I'll leave you, Sheila. He's sulking. He's not going to open his eyes while I'm here. I'll get you a cup of tea.'

Sheila was angry with them all for being so vindictive; she had grown accustomed to the Dublin way of keeping things pleasant on the surface.

'So you came, Sheila. I was afraid you wouldn't.' His voice made her heart jump because it had not changed; its vigour belied his pose. 'Take off your coat,' he told her and, when she had done so and laid it guiltily over the back of her chair, he asked her, 'Why didn't you come to see me before?'

'Should I have?' she asked, feeling her way.

'Didn't you hear I was hurt in an explosion? Everyone here knew about it.'

'I was told your injuries were slight. Then the children got measles and I forgot about it.' She told him the exact truth even though she knew it belittled him.

'You have children? Of course that explains what's happened to you. You've got quite thick through the middle. Such a waste – to go hiding yourself in a suburb in Dublin with a safe husband and little family. But you always were a very timorous person. You could have had a marvellous life – we could have gone to London, Paris, Amsterdam.'

'And then, when you would have tired of me?'

'Then you would have been a wonderful woman. You could have loved anybody.'

Sheila laughed. 'That's all an aberration, a perversion.'

'Sanctimonious as ever,' he said.

She shook her head, wondering how much he saw behind the dark glasses. 'My function in life is to be a comfort to my husband, to bring up my children, to see that the house is warm in the evening, that there is jam in the cupboard and bread in the bin, to clothe my children "in double garments".' She smiled to herself, feeling contentment in defining it. 'Can you see? Were your eyes damaged?' She thought she'd better show an interest in him.

'My eyes escaped.'

'Why do you wear those glasses, then? I can't see you at all.'

'I was cut by flying glass. I have scars. I don't like to look at them in the mirror so I have no intention of inflicting the sight of them on other people. But I can see you perfectly well.'

'And your legs? Can you walk?'

'I can limp. I refuse to. I have seen unfortunates who have been kneecapped. I will not be like them. I will not be mistaken for one of them.'

His mother came in carrying a tray. 'Do you hear him! There's not one thing to prevent him getting up and walking about and going out and finding a job again. His father came home from the war in 1945 with a limp but it didn't stop him working. He was a tailor – with the name Taylor. It's hard to believe, but his parents thought it a joke to get him into the tailoring. Still, it worked out all right for him, especially after the war. It wouldn't do for Paul, of course. Do you remember the way you used to rage when he'd hang the measuring-tape round your neck? He only did it to tease you, but such tempers! Engineering doesn't seem so useful when you're lame.' She lifted a squat table, rope-edged, glass-topped, and put it beside Paul's chair. She turned back to Sheila. 'He was killed by a motorbike that ran up on the footpath. I don't know what he'd say if he saw this carry-on. It's all pride. He's as proud as a peacock.'

Sheila looked from one to the other, seeing the resemblance in the perfect features that were a bit too strong for a woman's face.

'Weren't you the lucky girl wouldn't have him, Sheila. Look what you'd be saddled with now. I heard you saying you had children. Well he'd be the biggest and most spoilt of them – that's all he'd be to you.'

'Paul never asked me to marry him,' Sheila said, thinking she must leave things straight. 'I would have, if he'd asked me.'

They both smiled, Paul and his mother, congratulating each

other, before his mother said, 'More fool he then, but you had somebody's prayers.' She fussed over the china and teaspoons. Paul got up suddenly and hobbled across the room in such an ungainly way that Sheila had to lower her eyelids to ward off pain. As soon as he was out of the room his mother put her hand on Sheila's arm and her face was worried. 'Sheila, tell him to get out and about. Tell him to marry Eithne – she'd be good to him. He'll heed you. You should have heard the way he went on until I found your phone number and you said you'd come. He must think a lot of you. He doesn't pay any attention to me.'

Sheila shook her head. 'I never told Paul what to do. He told me. And if I could manage at all I did as he said. It was one of the things I loved about him.'

Mrs Taylor said, 'Oh well,' and for the rest of the afternoon, whether Paul was there or not, told all the details of the explosion that hit Paul passing by, and of the medical aftermath. Sheila was fraught with a feeling of uselessness. She wanted to put out her hand to him but feared it would be misinterpreted. When the yellow Volkswagen appeared in the street and sounded its horn, Mrs Taylor went out to get Sheila's coat which she had tidied away. Paul stood up, apparently straight and well, and putting his arm round Sheila's shoulders kissed her firmly. He smiled as her breath came out tremblingly. She felt she was being reclaimed. She wondered did their silhouette show to Eithne waiting in the car. Her heart was still shaking her ribs when she seated herself in the rapidly filling train. 'I'll be all right,' she thought, 'when I see Donal again. He'll put everything straight.' She remembered thinking the same thing after the birth of each baby when she was similarly dispirited and confused.

The train was crowded and noisy. People laughed and talked in northern accents and hailed one another with delight. Each carried a small piece of luggage. Sheila puzzled about them until a nun beside her explained that they had had jobs in Dublin for some years and visited their parents in Belfast some weekends. 'They have gone where the life is,' she said, sighing.

'It's a pity,' Sheila said. 'Belfast must miss them.'

'Belfast offered them nothing,' the nun said. 'I had to leave because the numbers of children went down. I'm teaching in Dublin because there are plenty of children there so far.'

'All the same, Belfast was a nice place,' Sheila said.

'A place to look back on fondly when you're safely out of it. A grim deadly town. Good kindly people, but the place grinds them down.'

Crossing the border the nun said, 'Don't you feel you can relax better when it's all behind you?' Sheila was angry with her for putting it into words. The evening sun filled the carriage with golden light and a boy, banging the padding of his seat, raised a cloud of transfigured dust. The ticket collector spoke sternly to him and the boy took it meekly, laughing when he was gone.

Donal's anxious face met her at the barrier. 'Sheila, are you all right?'

'Of course I am. Why wouldn't I be?' She took his arm.

'That letter,' he said, and she, having forgotten it, scoffed, 'Ach! The letter.' Glad in the security of the car, they smiled at each other as they drove through streets filled with strolling crowds. Sheila said it had been raining and grey in Belfast. Donal told her about his evening with the children in the park. They had seen a squirrel.

'I've never seen a squirrel,' Sheila said.

'Have you not! God, that's terrible, Sheila. Isn't it a pity you weren't with us this evening. We'll go back next week, will we? We could just see it, you know, up in the tree with little webby claws holding on to a branch. Only we couldn't watch it in peace because young brats came along and started throwing stones to make it move. I shouted at them. Then the two girls scolded me for my language so we left. They told me the neighbours would not let them play with their children if they knew I used such words.'

He laughed, and Sheila laughed because he did, but she wasn't listening to him. She was wishing she had been with them, wishing she had not gone to Belfast, had not seen that bulldozed street, had not met Eithne or Paul's mother, had not closed her eyes against Paul's hobbling. She thought of the green of the park and of children running, laughing, and the sun shafting through the trees so that the warmth on her back would bring, as it always did, the impulse of thankfulness. They were nearly home. Sheila could see the rounded sedate hills with their planted forests and the featherbed and their winding roads with streams of lamplit cars. Teenaged cyclists circled lazily on the footpath. Children's window blinds were pulled, shutting out the end of the day.

Sheila pushed open their own front door and noticed the trail of children's fingermarks on the wallpaper the whole length of the stairs, the shoemarks on the skirting boards and the places on the doors where prams and pushchairs had chipped out actual lumps of wood. She must deal with it, she thought. When the baby-sitter left she heard Malachy's bedroom door open and his still-clumsy footsteps coming down. He trotted in shouting, 'Mammy, Mammy, Mammy, what did you bring me?' She gathered him up in her arms. '"I have brought you myself," cried Moses with a sly look.' She said it because her mother used to say that in similar circumstances, quoting from an old schoolbook in her grand-mother's time, but as she spoke she looked over her son's head clasped warm on her shoulders and smiled into her husband's careful eyes. When the child was back in bed and Donal held out his arms for her, she put her hands on his shoulders but, when she saw her fingers grimed from the journey gripping him, she deliberately slackened her hold for fear he should ever be pulled into the shade of those black northern cliffs.

The Cypress Trees

The Cypress Trees

G avin hurried home from school, half running, lopsided with the heavy schoolbag under one arm. Beyond the roundabout the whole sky was black and down the road to the west the big new church in another estate stood out against the cloud like the prow of an ocean-going liner. At the corner of his own road he stopped and searched in the front pocket of his jeans until he felt the comfort of the door key and kept it clenched in his hand. He had another key in his pencil case to be on the safe side but he never liked to delay on the doorstep. That woman who had come to live in the 'granny flat' in the house opposite was forever at her window, watching with her pale-blue eyes in that very white face. She made Gavin uncomfortable. Anyway, he never relaxed when neighbour women asked him to come in and wait in their houses until his parents came home from work. The children who lived nearby were either younger than his eleven years, or girls, and although he didn't mind playing with them outside it was a different matter indoors. Their mothers had a habit of making them do their homework when he was there, or they gave him things to eat he didn't like – bread with margarine, for instance, or tea with too

much milk in it. He liked to close his own front door behind
him.

He stopped in the hall to pick up the post – a couple of
business envelopes and a strange crumpled-looking letter with
unfamiliar writing addressed to his mother. He put them on
the hall table and stood looking in the mirror above it. 'Your
writing, Gavin Mac Evoy, is atrocious!' he told his reflection,
imitating his teacher. 'You'll never pass the test into St Mark's
College at this rate.' Trouble showed in his grey eyes for a
moment but he shrugged off his worry, pulled off his hat and
with his hand smoothed his light hair back into shape. The
last time that had come up – when his Christmas report arrived
– he had said to his parents, 'What will happen if I don't get
into St Mark's? What am I going to do?'

His father had said, 'Of course you'll get in. You have plenty
of ability,' and his mother had said, 'We have two pay-packets
in this house and only one of a family – we can afford to pay
for you in one of the colleges outside the free scheme.'

'My friends will all be going to St Mark's but I'll not know
anybody in these other places.'

'If your friends can get in, you can get in if you put your
mind to it,' his mother snapped.

'It's not like that, Mum,' he explained. 'The teacher draws
names out of a hat.'

'Don't be ridiculous,' his mother said. 'You can't expect us
to believe that.'

'It's true,' he insisted. 'I'm telling you. That's what happened last year. We all do the exam and if forty pass and
there's only room for twenty they pull twenty names out of a
hat.'

'How, then,' his mother asked, 'are your friends any more
certain than you of getting in?'

'Ah, well they're different,' he said. 'If you have a brother already in St Mark's you get in all right. They all have brothers.'

His father had looked miserable then, and his mother cross, because they all remembered the time not so long ago that he had raged and cried and banged his head on the door when he heard that his friend Brian's mother had a new baby boy, giving him three brothers, when he, Gavin, had none. Later that night he had heard his mother shouting that she would not be having any more children, she didn't care about Gavin or his father or anybody else, nor would she adopt any either. She was happy going out to work and she wasn't changing. She wasn't going to be like *her* mother, having seven one after the other and slaving away at dressmaking in that poky little front room in a corporation house because her father had a 'bad back' and would only work occasionally. Gavin rarely saw any of these people because his mother, having pushed herself away from their poverty, wanted to have nothing to do with them.

His own house was warm and comfortable. He knew there would be food left for him in the kitchen but he didn't really want it. He wasn't interested in food. He was thin, especially his legs, so that he would never wear shorts, even on hot days, but sweltered in his jeans. The sudden blatter of rain on the window brought him into the front room to look out at the long rods of rain scudding the road. Some straggling homecomers turned their backs to the force of it and put their schoolbags on their heads. There'd be no football for a while. As the concrete darkened the road emptied. There used to be a bus rattling down at irregular intervals until the chairman of the residents' committee asked to have it diverted. Gavin liked the whoosh it used to make as it tore down if the road was clear. He liked it even better if it couldn't pass parked cars and sat hooting until someone appeared from a house half running, rattling car keys and contrived a space. Now there was no excitement and since that Christmas report he wasn't allowed to turn on the television except at weekends. He was to do his homework after school and they would hear his tables, spellings, etc. after dinner. Sometimes they did and sometimes they forgot. Sometimes they were quite sharp with him and sometimes they said, yawning, 'Oh I suppose it'll do.'

The room held nothing for him as he turned from the window. The mushroom-coloured couch and chairs at one end and the glass-topped dining table beyond the sliding doors were all immaculate. His own feet had made slight scuffmarks on the pale carpet. His mother tidied and polished every night before she went to bed. He trailed up to his own room with his schoolbag and put out his homework. He did a sum but his pen began to leak messily. He put it down and leaned his chair backwards, trying to see how far he could tilt before having to grab at the table to prevent falling. When that palled he banged around the small room in time to his transistor and then flung himself on his bed to bounce.

He jumped up when he heard his parents' car and straightened the Manchester United duvet. At the window he was just in time to glimpse his mother's shiny brown hair and shiny brown boots. He was always proud looking at her compared to some of the mothers he saw wearing slippers in the house, sometimes rollers in their hair. She was frowning over her letter as he came down the stairs smiling. She lifted her eyes and glared at Gavin and passed the letter to his father who read it quickly and then said, 'The thing to do with anonymous letters is put them in the fire.'

'Let Gavin read it first and see what he says,' his mother said.

Gavin took the blue lined notepaper and puzzled over the writing with its long unfamiliar loops. When he got used to that, the message was clear enough: this person signed 'The Watcher' was accusing him of stealing from shops. The recollection, never far from his mind, of taking a Yorkie bar in the shop beside the school for no reason except the impulse of the moment made his mother point to his face. 'Look at him! Just look at him. He's the picture of guilt.' She grabbed his shoulder and shook him. 'What have you stolen? How long has this been going on? Where did you take these things?' When he staggered back and sat down on the stairs she hit his head and when he put his hands up over his head for protection she hit his hands and arms.

His father said, 'Angela, go easy. You'll hurt him. I'm sure it's not serious.'

His father was a fool. Of course it was serious, he thought – the trouble he'd had putting it back afterwards.

His mother stepped back and straightened her suit. 'Do you want a thief for a son?' she demanded. 'What did you steal, you little runt?'

Gavin closed his lips tight and wouldn't answer either her ranting or his father's pleading. She threatened to tell the police, the school, the shops, so that they would all know he was a thief. Then suddenly she turned her back on him and shouted, 'Oh get out of my sight. Go to your room and don't let me see you again. Go, go, go!' He ran up the stairs, tripping at the top, stumbled into his room and closed the door.

He stood for a long time in the middle of the small room with his hands up to his head. 'She hit me,' he said to himself, enraged. There was no space in him for any other thought.

He had taken the bar of chocolate on a February day that had started fine and had turned windy and grey. He had shivered without hat or gloves waiting to pay for the bunch of parsley his mother had asked him to buy on the way home from school. He put the chocolate in his pocket and ran home laughing to himself. When he took it out in the house and looked at it in the palm of his hand he wondered what had come over him. He had plenty of pocket money; if he had wanted to buy chocolate there was nothing to prevent him. He was not tempted to eat it. In fact he felt if he ate it he would be sick. He put it into his schoolbag, meaning to put it back on the shelf the next day. He knew about restitution from his grandfather – his father's father.

He had been a bricklayer and one of his favourite stories was about a man from the country who went to Confession and said, 'Father, I stole a house,' because he'd taken bricks, blocks, tiles and cement from his employer and suppliers over the months and built his house with his own labour. His grandfather used to chuckle, telling about the difficulties the man had encountered for the rest of his life, saving up and buying materials and smuggling them back until his conscience was clear and he'd said, 'Now I won't have to go to God arguing.'

So Gavin knew he had to put the chocolate back but he hadn't realised how hard it would be to slip away by himself without his schoolfriends, to poke down under his books for the hidden bar, becoming daily more battered, only to be prevented by the shopowners or hovering customers from going near the sweet stand. After each attempt he felt more like a thief, he felt everybody knew to look at him that he was a thief, and he slunk home in distress. Eventually he had managed and then he avoided the shop completely. He wished that his grandfather could have turned it into just a funny story but his grandfather had had a heart attack, or, as his mother put it, 'a massive coronary', and took no further interest in the world outside his own chest.

Not that his grandfather had ever talked to Gavin. When Gavin and his father had gone across the town to visit him, as they did some Sunday afternoons, he had shaken hands and said, 'Hello, young man. How are you?' Gavin said, 'Well,' and that was the end of the conversation. After that Gavin sat listening, snug in the old-fashioned kitchen with a coal fire and a red shiny floor and a table and chairs, unlike his mother's with its breakfast bar and stools and units. His grandfather had a wooden armchair at one side of the fire, his grandmother a lumpy cushioned one at the other. She sat Gavin at the table and gave him lemonade and biscuits. His father and grandfather each had a bottle of stout although his grand-mother frequently urged them not to drink that terrible stuff but to have a nice glass of whiskey instead. They would all laugh and she would show photographs of her daughters' children and tell how well they were doing in their exams and at their music and dancing lessons. Gavin's mother complained that his grandmother took no interest in him, caring only for her daughters' children, but Gavin loved hearing about these wonderful cousins. He relished his connection with their suc-cesses. After his grandfather came home from hospital he sat sunk in himself, listening to his own breathing, sighing, while his wife sat on the edge of her shapeless chair, watching him, ready to jump if he needed her. Their visits were curtailed; they were too tiring for his grandfather, it was no place for a child.

Because his arms were aching in their strained position Gavin took his hands from his head but he still stood in the middle of the floor. Cooking smells reached his room. His mother was quick and skilled at contriving the meal – she did much of the preparation the night before. He could hear her voice, sharp at times, and his father's, lower, placating. He expected them to call him down any minute and he tried to make up his mind if he should tell them what had happened or stay silent. He had no guarantee they would believe him.

Eventually he realised they were leaving him alone. They would not have him at the table. They would not eat with him. He curled up on the bed with his boots out over the side, and because he shivered he pulled the cover over himself and fell asleep.

His father at his own bedtime peeped in and, seeing the child's sleeping face on the pillow but not the boots still on, decided that Gavin had taken himself to bed and that it would be better not to disturb him. The closing door wakened Gavin although he didn't know what woke him or for a moment what he was doing in bed, hot and sticky in his clothes. He thought at first he had flu, but then he remembered. He lay wide awake in the darkness listening to his parents talking companionably together, laughing a little now and then. When the house was silent except for the clicking of contracting heat he felt a pain in his stomach. He thought it was likely hunger so he got up and went down to the fridge, not taking any particular care to keep quiet. He took out a pint of milk and drank straight from the bottle, a habit that his mother said belonged to 'the lowest of the low'. He ate a banana and left the skin lying on the counter. Then he opened the back door and went out.

The rain had stopped during the evening and the air was sweet, perfumed by the apple blossoms in one garden and lilac and wallflowers in another. The sky was clear, moonlit, showing the unbroken lawn in his own garden as smooth as the sitting-room carpet. He walked along the high end wall that separated the gardens of his road from those of the back road. He held his arms out to balance like a tightrope walker, except when he could catch on to trees or bushes that people had planted to hide the bare concrete blocks. A grey cat met him, then turned and went ahead of him on the wall with its tail erect. Gavin smiled, following it over a garage and down with a jump to the road. He kept to the shady part of the footpath, aware that if he met one of the policemen who patrolled the district he would have to account for himself. At the foot of the back road there were new houses, half a dozen of them unoccupied. He headed for them. They were expensive houses but just before they were finished the builder had disappeared, bankrupt, leaving them without plumbing or fireplaces. They had deep sheltered porches and Gavin knew that, night after night, bigger boys went there to smoke and play cards while their parents thought they were at the youth club. He had watched the group in fascination the previous summer and they had repeatedly chased him. They were all gone home to bed now, so he pressed himself into a corner among their litter of cigarette ends and empty bottles. Even in the shelter he was cold without a jacket. The milk and banana were cold in his stomach. An animal howl of misery gathered in him but he checked it and ran.

He took a different wall home, hugging his arms round his cold jersey, leaving his balance to luck. When he staggered and fell off into someone's rhubarb bed he picked himself up. The house was in darkness. He got as far as the kitchen window but he found it too high for him to reach so he pulled the dustbin over underneath the sill. Fat red worms wriggled in the exposed wet circle. He stood on the bin lid and surveyed the window. He had heard that if you tapped persistently with the heel of your shoe on the metal frame of the little top window it would spring open. But his were expensive French padded boots with thick spongy soles, useless for that purpose. He jumped down and hunted on the ground for an implement. The worms were disappearing behind the coal bunker. He saw the head of a small hammer, possibly a child's. It had no handle but he climbed back with it and tapped awkwardly. He thought the blows were far too light to have any effect, and almost laughed out loud when the window sprang and he was able to catch the opening and haul himself close to the glass. He stretched his right arm in until he could knock open the handle of the bigger window and he stood there looking in, the whole room at his mercy in the moonlight. He pushed aside a teapot and an egg-timer and put his foot in on the painted wood. There was still warmth in the kitchen and he thought of coming in until he could face the cold again. A dark armchair had a comfortable bulk.

Then the floorboards upstairs creaked and a light went on in the window above him. He stayed without moving. On the ledge beside his foot was a metal tea-caddy and the lid held three magnets, two little fancy ones with handles and the other a solid horseshoe, worn, partly red. He pulled it off and the tin rattled slightly. He held the magnet in the palm of his hand, liking it, and then closed his fingers over it so that it felt like his door key, only heavier. Someone was struggling with the upstairs window but he was able to hide in the only shadow near the house before the bathroom window was flung wide and a stout woman in a dressing-gown looked out, craning from one side to the other. His shelter was given by a cordon of branchy slanting trees, trained along wires held by poles. The ground where he crouched had been recently dug and black soil mulched in. A mixture of terror and excitement had Gavin's bowel in a ferment so that he pushed down his trousers and emptied it on the ground. He hunkered in the same place, disgust in abeyance, even though the window had been shut again and the light was switched off.

Two motorbikes roared, one after the other, on the main road. The noise and the speed vibrated through his head. He'd get a motorbike as soon as he could. There'd be more scope with a motorbike. His father would buy it for him to make up for his unhappiness. Listening as the machines faded in the distance he had a wild hope that he'd find release in hurtling power and swinging light and ringing sound. He became aware of his squatting position and he straightened up, fixing his clothes carefully, and stepped to one side. He looked at the magnet on his open hand. He was keeping that. He wasn't giving it back. He took out his door key and laid it beside the magnet. They remained separate. Disappointed, he put them both in his pocket. He'd go home, in the back door, wash himself and go to bed. If his parents asked him any questions he'd stay silent. He plotted out the best way to his house.

All along the back walls of these gardens people had planted cypress trees to give them privacy from newer, cheaper bungalows on the road behind. The trees cut into the moonlit sky. One section was carefully clipped and tended, to form a manageable light-green hedge. Other trees soared, pristine, pointed, giving a dark nesting-room for magpies or a swaying perch for pigeons. But, from where Gavin stood in the soft soil among the cordons, the row that blocked his view had been carelessly hacked and chopped, irremediably mutilated.

Sudden Infant Death

Sudden Infant Death

I t was a beautiful sunny morning with a clear blue sky and a pink and white blur of cherry blossom on the trees that lined the road. 'I remember this road when it was the bleakest in Dublin before these trees were planted,' an older woman said. 'Just straight east-west and the cars speeding along it.' Jenny said she hadn't been living here as long as that. 'And of course,' the woman went on, 'there'll come a cold rainy day and the trees will be stripped and the blossoms will blow along the footpath so we'd better appreciate it while we can.' She turned in at her gate and Jenny came on to her own quieter narrower road.

The postman on his bicycle saluted her as he rode away after his delivery. She had seen him in the distance earlier while she was bringing four-year-old Sarah to school, but she got few letters. There was one in the porch now, addressed to her.

'Dear Jenny,' she read.

'Do the guards know you murdered little Rory by holding his face down under the water? They say you got depressed because you were expecting again but that is no excuse, is it? I will write soon.

'A Watcher'

She crumpled the letter in horror, but then she thought she'd better show it to Matt. She smoothed the page and put it on the cabinet beside their bed. They would need to move again, she told herself. They'd moved away from their first house as soon as Sarah was born; it hadn't seemed necessary while she was pregnant but after the birth she had insisted on leaving although she loved the place. Matt had been mystified but she said, 'They know we couldn't look after Ruairi right. Well we didn't, did we? So they'll be keeping an eye on Sarah all the time and I'd be so ashamed.' He thought they should consider it for a while but she'd banged the table and shouted at him and he'd set about selling the house and buying this one with all the trouble and expense of a hurry to buy and a delay in selling. Aoife had been four then and only just settled into school and she'd had to be re-settled as Sarah would now. They wouldn't want to go. The children had their friends and Matt had planted fruit trees in the garden and done all kinds of things to the house. But she wouldn't stay if everyone knew about Ruairi, even though this was the only mention she'd ever heard.

Matt drove home for his lunch because this house wasn't too far from his work and because he wanted to prevent her growing sad during the day. She showed him the letter and before he had a chance to read it she said, 'We have to move again.'

'Because of this?' he exclaimed. 'Some ill-natured unfortunate has got hold of a garbled account of Ruairi's death. We'll ignore it or else bring it to the police.'

She snatched it from him and tore it in bits. 'I never want to have anything to do with the guards again,' she said and began to cry.

Matt put his arm round her and sighed. He'd married a girl who dressed smartly, laughed at his jokes and threw her arms round his neck, to kiss him for no reason at all. Sometimes he thought she was recovering but then one of the little girls would get sick or complain about school and she would stop eating, look anxious and lose weight till her clothes hung loose on her. He had expected that she would be better after Sarah was born but the opposite had happened. Matt himself missed his small son because he had been a lively child and *his* child, but he could not understand why it should cloud their whole future life.

'I'll be late going back to work,' he said, sitting down at the table, and, still sniffing, she served his lunch and picked at her own.

'Eat your meat anyway,' he told her, trying to make her laugh because that was what she said to the children, but she ignored him. She didn't even get up from the table to see him to the door. When she went out to meet Sarah at two o'clock at the school gate she neglected to comb her hair or renew her lipstick. She held Sarah tightly by the hand but she took no notice when Sarah said, 'Mammy, Mammy, look – it's snowing?' In the east wind the petals were drifting up the road and lying in heaps in the gutters.

They had been on their summer holidays at the seaside when Ruairi disappeared. It was a chilly grey day and after lunchtime Jenny had been listless, feeling heavy with her pregnancy and swollen legs. After shopping for food they'd all been at the beach in the morning and she had come back early across the railway line to their rented chalet so that she could wash out the children's clothes and have the meal ready when they came home. When she said, 'Look at my feet,' Matt easily persuaded her to have a rest in bed while he looked after the children on the beach. After a while Aoife complained of the cold and insisted on going back to the car for her jacket. Matt tried to talk her out of it because of the danger of the railway line, but she was a strong-willed child. He left two-year-old Ruairi on the rug where he was arranging pebbles in lines. When they came back he was gone.

Matt thought he'd gone towards the car so they gathered the rug, buckets, spades, sandals and balls and headed back there. There was no sign of him so they dumped the stuff in and Matt put Aoife up on his shoulders, hoping her sharp eyes would spot him on the strand among the huddled families or the scattered football players. At teatime he brought Aoife back to the chalet and had to report to Jenny that Ruairi couldn't be found.

'I'll get him,' she said impatiently to hide from herself her panic, but Matt said no, he'd go out again by himself. She had to stay there in case Ruairi came home. She couldn't go rushing around – it would add to their troubles. When darkness threatened he checked with Jenny and then told the police that their two-year-old son had been lost on the strand. They said there was little they could do at night – there was a high tide that left little of the strand dry. It was a pity they hadn't been informed earlier. They'd enquire at the houses in the little town. They'd get word out on the radio. Did he know anybody hereabouts? Had he made friends? Had anybody approached him?

Aoife was anxious. 'Sure it wasn't my fault, Mammy? I wasn't minding him. Wasn't it Daddy that was minding him? I was cold, Mammy. I needed my anorak. You always said I wasn't to get cold.' Jenny automatically reassured her, although her teeth wanted to clench and she found it difficult to react to the child. When she eventually was put to sleep Jenny sat in the dark waiting for Matt. He went to bed but she wouldn't go. He said he'd be up at first light and he needed his sleep. She did too, he said. There was no sense in sitting up but if she refused to come to bed there was nothing he could do about it. He was asleep in five minutes.

She was cold in the chair. She could have got Ruairi's blanket off his empty bed but she couldn't bring herself to do that. It was his own blanket from home so that it had the baby-powder smell that hung over his cot. Throughout the day he was an active, troublesome two year old. There was no rest for anyone while he was around. During her pregnancy she had often wished that someone would take him off her hands for half an hour during the afternoon so that she could put her feet up. She had complained to Matt that nobody ever thought of relieving her, nobody ever helped her. Other pregnant women had sisters or mothers but neither she nor Matt had anybody in Dublin. Ruairi banged about the house. He jumped from the couch to the floor. He threw things. He hid things. He turned on taps. He emptied the washing-up liquid. He couldn't talk very well and he raged when he wasn't understood. When she was very tired Jenny thought to herself that she didn't really love him any more. Sitting stiff and cold in the seaside chalet, she realised she didn't love anybody any more, not Matt, nor Aoife nor Ruairi. She did what was needful for each of them when she wasn't too tired but she looked on them as encumbrances, all demanding attention. Matt did offer to help, as he had this afternoon when Ruairi disappeared, but she saw him give her a cold look every now and again, not a bit affectionate, just because she was dull and tired and cross. And now here was this extra trouble that she shouldn't have to deal with – Ruairi going and losing himself because Matt wasn't careful enough. Her mind was slipping slightly out of control although she thought herself wide awake.

She opened her eyes with the early-morning light at the window and saw Matt putting on his clothes. She struggled out of the chair, her back and legs aching. 'I'll get a breakfast,' she said. 'You'll need it.' When he came into the kitchen the reality of the situation struck her. 'Oh Matt,' she said, putting her hands on his chest.

He hugged her. 'I'll find him, love,' he told her. 'I promise you.' He looked strained, not refreshed, after his sleep.

'He's dead. Ruairi is dead.' She realised but she didn't say that. She had to get used to the certainty herself before imposing it on Matt.

They found his body at the far end of the beach where the sand ended in outcrops of grassy turf with knee-deep channels between them. He was lying on his front with his head to one side as he had lain in his cot with his arms tucked in underneath him. The only footprints were his own where, according to the guards, he had been jumping backwards and forwards from one tussock to the other before he lay down and was covered in his sleep by the incoming tide.

A doctor came to the chalet with the guard to break the news to Jenny. He held on to her as the guard talked. She was aware of a strange man with his hand on her bare arm. She insisted on being brought straight away to see Ruairi's little body although they all advised against it. 'Matt,' she exclaimed. 'He hadn't even got his jersey on.' And her heart broke at the thought of him cold. But the guards fussed at the mention of his jersey and Matt couldn't tell if he'd had it on at the beach or not. They had to go back to the chalet to find it bundled up with the rug they'd used. Jenny couldn't understand and didn't care what that was all about, nor why they asked her if she'd been out of the chalet during the afternoon while Matt and Aoife hunted for Ruairi.

'Sure that's why he got lost,' she said several times. 'It was because I took a rest. I should never have taken a rest. I'll never take a rest again.'

When they were gone Jenny sat down and Matt knelt in front of her. 'I'm sorry,' he said. 'I'm no use. But I love you, Jenny, and I'll do everything I can to look after you and Aoife and the new baby. I do love you.'

She pressed his head down on her knees and stroked his hair. 'I love you too,' she would have said, only her tongue was too tired to lift up the words.

And in the time that followed they were never said. There was an inquest at which the coroner offered sympathy, Ruairi was buried and Sarah was born, and they moved house. Aoife had to be constantly consoled about Ruairi's death.

'He can't talk right, Mammy,' she said, day after day. 'He needs me with him to tell people what he's saying.'

Jenny assured her Ruairi was happy in heaven.

'He won't know anybody there. He'll have no friends – only old people go to heaven.' When Jenny told her that lots of children were there she began to worry that she would die too and refused to go to sleep for fear her breathing would stop. 'Mammy, won't you listen all night to see I'm still breathing.'

The change to a new neighbourhood put an extra strain on Aoife with the loss of her friends. Jenny could do nothing but hug her and try to interest her in Sarah, but until Sarah was past the age at which Ruairi died Aoife kept her distance. Then they played together, with their dolls and the children who lived nearby.

Jenny herself eventually got over the wrenching pain at her heart every time she thought of Ruairi's wild energy. Why hadn't she appreciated and enjoyed it? When Sarah was at that age she wondered how she could ever have objected to Ruairi's mischief and she cried often, thinking of it. The crying seemed

85

to soften the pain. Nothing alleviated the guilt. Frequently when she had seated her two little girls at the table and called Matt to his meal she had the feeling that there was another one missing. It wasn't Ruairi. It was just a child, maybe upstairs or outside. And at night, if Matt mentioned that they could relax because the children were safe in bed, she had the impulse to say, 'No, they're not, not all.' She didn't say it. How could she explain this floating intimation of a child waiting to be gathered into the family?

The doorbell rang and a neighbour, Sheila Ryan, stood there. 'Can I come in?' she asked. 'I saw you at the school but you were looking at nobody. Then you disappeared so quickly I didn't get a chance to speak to you. Is there something wrong?'

'I think I'm getting the flu or something. I'm a bit depressed,' Jenny said, with her back to her while she put on the kettle.

'I just wondered,' Sheila said. 'A few people round here have got nasty letters.'

'Letters?' Jenny said, turning round before she could stop herself.

'You tell me and then I'll tell you,' Sheila said, and then because Jenny looked so stricken she said, 'We'll reverse that. You know I come from Belfast?' Jenny smiled because Sheila's accent was still strong. 'Well I was going up there to visit an old acquaintance last Sunday, but a few days before that I got a letter saying I had been mixed up in violence and that I was to stay out of Belfast or they'd get me.'

'But you went?' Jenny said. 'You weren't afraid? What did Donal say?'

'Oh he was in a state,' Sheila laughed. 'But he did the right thing. He took the letter to the police. What did you do with yours?'

'I burned it,' Jenny said. 'I tore it up when Matt wanted to bring it to the garda station.'

'That's what has you in bad form,' Sheila said. She drank her tea. 'I must go. Maeve O'Reilly is keeping an eye on the children but you know what Malachy is like. Nobody but a mother could mind him for long. Do you want to tell me what the letter was about?' Sheila was always direct.

'It was about Ruairi,' Jenny said.

'Your little boy that was drowned before you came here?' Sheila said. 'That's what I thought.'

'How did you know about Ruairi?' Jenny asked in dismay.

'Well we all knew about it at the time because it was in the papers and on the radio and we all had great sympathy for the child's family without knowing who it was. Then when you moved in here we just wanted to make you feel better. Except whoever is writing those letters, of course.'

'I thought nobody knew,' Jenny said. 'I never mentioned it.'

'There are no secrets in Ireland,' Sheila laughed. 'People always know. I'm away! It's a pity you destroyed the letter but Matt should tell the police anyway.'

Coming home from his work Matt was thinking he had been mad to saddle himself with a wife and children when he might have been still carefree in an apartment on his own and girlfriends anytime he wanted them. It was too late to think about that now, but one thing he could insist on. He was not moving. He was not giving in any more to Jenny's hysteria. His face was grim when he appeared at six o'clock but Jenny said at once, 'You were right about not moving. It seems everybody knew about us all along and didn't think any the worse of us.' She expected him to hug her, or at least smile at her, but he said, 'I'm glad you're not so mopy,' and standing with his back to the radiator opened up the evening paper.

'Mopy?' she repeated. 'What do you mean – mopy? It's a bit more than that I've been through. I think I had every reason to be upset. I'm sorry if I'm not always the life and soul of the party.'

'I think I'll go away for a holiday,' he said. 'Just by myself. If I can get a cheap flight to the Canaries or Portugal. I've never been to those places. Or Greece.'

'And what about us?' Jenny asked. 'What about our holiday?'

'We don't go on holidays any more,' he said. 'Or haven't you noticed?'

The children were in the sitting-room. She could hear the television. She hoped they weren't listening.

'I was afraid,' she said quietly. 'Surely you can understand that.'

'I've done my best,' Matt said. 'Nobody could say I wasn't sympathetic but I can't stand this gloom. I want things to be happy. When I turn the car into this road every day I wonder what kind of mood you'll be in, whether it'll be all right for me to be cheerful or if I have to be depressed all evening.'

'All right,' she said. 'I know what you mean. I should keep up a good front here, as well as outside. I'll change. You go on your holiday and when you come back you'll never hear another word of complaint out of me about anything. Ever.'

He looked uncomfortable. She laid the table, turned on the radio, called the children in for their tea, chatting to them brightly. While they ate she included him in the conversation, trying to put him at his ease, as if he were an awkward visitor. When the two little girls were in bed she sat on the edge of her own bed and thought of the effort it would take on her part to make Matt happy again. He would not go away on a holiday alone. She knew that. But she had to behave in a way she had never done. She had always accepted that he loved her and relied on that unthinkingly. She thought of how she'd jeered at advice in magazines about 'working at your marriage'. That, she decided, was what she had to do. Maybe she'd be successful. Maybe she'd even console herself in the process. Maybe when the children, whatever number there were, grew up she would not care any more and he would have to take life as it happened. But now, dependent, she would pander to his wishes. She was resolute. She felt forlorn.

Under Control

Under Control

My dear Peggy,

The other day my next-door neighbour told me about a quarrel with her sister as a result of which she wrote a letter, twenty-five pages long, to her daughter doing a Ph.D in Seattle, Washington. Here I am writing this to my sister married in Oxford about my daughter who will never get a Ph.D in Seattle or anywhere else. Why do I burden you with this? I remember when Mother told me about her worries I used to say to myself, 'Why does she pile it all on me? What's wrong with her talking to Father?' I normally talk things over with Owen, you know that, but, when I see the looks of dislike that he gives his beloved daughter nowadays, I can't say a word to him about her. I know you love her and will be able to separate fact from reality in what I tell you. And she loves you far more than she does me. 'Do you know how much I hate you?' she asked me this morning. It was no shock to me, but I didn't like to hear it said. I told her I knew she didn't like me and that it was a pity because I loved her, always loved her, that she was especially dear to me, being our first baby after the little one that died. She told me then that

I was telling lies, that I never thought much of her, that I'd hated her since before Susan was born.

I know you're thinking that with Susan two years old now we should all have adapted to the way things have turned out, but a letter came on the morning's post – an anonymous letter. It threatened that Susan's mother, having realised that I was above the legal age to be given a child to adopt, was going to apply to the Courts to have Susan returned to her. I can't think who wrote it. I haven't given my mind to that yet. Stella was still at the breakfast table in her dressing-gown, face not washed, hair not brushed. I can never get her out in time for her early lectures. I handed her the letter and said, 'She's got hold of the wrong end of the stick, hasn't she?' Maybe it wasn't the most tactful thing to say but it always amuses me the way they question me about my letters – who wrote that, what has she to say, who are you writing to? It's the same with telephone calls, in spite of our giving them perfect privacy. We never say, 'What time were you in at last night?' but if I stop to talk to somebody coming home from the church there is a real inquisition. 'Where were you? Why were you not home long ago? What did you find to talk about so long?' That's why I handed over the letter, although indeed it's more Brian and David that want to keep me circumscribed. Stella doesn't take much interest any more. I try to be careful with her but it's impossible to weigh every word all the time.

She read it and gave it back and that's when she said did I know how much she hated me, that I had never given her any chance of making her own decisions, that I never stopped pushing her, that I had taken her child from her without giving her any option. Did I realise that St Augustine said the chief urge in us is to dominate and that I had never controlled that? She's studying philosophy in university so she throws this at me. Do you, living in Oxford, ever hear any chit-chat about

St Augustine and what he said, and what qualifications he has that we should heed anything he did say? Or do the physicists you move among not really care a lot about St Augustine? Perhaps that strange Torus of theirs concentrates their thoughts so that they have no ideas outside their task of seeking to create power by nuclear fusion rather than fission.

Did Stella ever tell you how she came to have the baby? She's fond of you and must be grateful to you – maybe she told you before now what she told me this morning. 'Told' is not a proper verb to describe her onslaught on me. She was shouting, yelling, until I warned her she'd waken Susan. All the time she looked at me with such detestation that I have to offload it. It's hard for me at this moment to remember the quiet polite girl Stella was all through school, no trouble to anyone and the nuns always telling me she was responsible and co-operative and that it didn't matter at all that her exam results were very mediocre. I used to think she was content – happy would be too strong a word. She didn't go out much, no dances, no boyfriends. I hoped going to the university would improve that but she just stayed with her schoolfriends and worried about her notes and her exams and her money. She was anxious to get a summer job so as to have her own money for the next year and when she got one in a kind of youth hotel in France we were all delighted. I thought it would help her French. She tells me now that I pushed her into taking it just to improve her French, that she was terrified going and that she was killed with loneliness while she was there and what she really wanted was to get into a shop or an office here at home. Her wicked mother threw her out of the nest and she hadn't spoken to a soul all the fortnight she was there before the Friday she telephoned us to find out if she had passed her first-year exams. She hadn't, you remember. Owen had gone over to the university and found that her name was not on the list of passes, but we didn't know how many subjects she had failed and wouldn't until Monday, so we hadn't rung her and hoped she wouldn't ring us, but she did, after dinner-time, and I had to tell her. I remember consoling her with the assurance that she'd get her repeat exams in September, that she should stay where she was until she heard how many subjects she had to repeat. This morning she said that I ordered her to stay where she was, that she'd just have to pass in September or she wouldn't be acceptable at home. She wanted to give up university, she says. She never wanted to go to university. She didn't enjoy studying. She was never any good at it. She hated not doing well in exams when Brian and David were so clever. All she wanted was to get a job and enjoy her own money and her freedom from books. But I was so determined to control her, to push her into things she had no wish for, that she had no chance to run her own life, so she just had the baby to force some change.

She had gone into the nearest town before dark because she was too depressed to stay in her room. By a strange chance she met a lad she'd known to see in college but not to speak to. He was cock-a-hoop because he had passed his final law exams and since he had nobody to celebrate with they went off together and ended up in his bed. When she went back to the hostel she scrubbed herself all over in disgust – every place he had touched, her teeth, her tongue, in horror of herself. Still, on Monday after she rang home and found out she had failed only French and I was insistent that she'd have no difficulty passing one subject in September, the only way out she could think of was to go back to this lad every evening for a week until he moved off to Switzerland. Now you may think this was confiding in me, but not if you'd heard her. It was as if I had arranged for her violation.

I had never allowed myself to wonder how or when it

happened. That would have been like reading a diary or her letters. Owen used to say many a time before the baby was born, 'Did she ever tell you how she came to do such a thing?' and I always said no but that I supposed it was because of loneliness, human nature and the skimpy clothes they wore in the heat. They certainly were not in love although maybe Stella was a bit dazzled by him. When she told him in September that she was pregnant he said he took no responsibility, that he was going on for the bar and could have no blemish on his character, and if she said anything he'd deny ever having spoken to her in his life. But you know that. It's all very well for her to say now that she deliberately decided to change her life, but I remember the pathetic picture she made when she told me just afterwards. She didn't know what to do, so it was as well I did in spite of all her talk of my being so domineering. And of course we couldn't have managed if you hadn't been living in England and prepared to take her until after the baby was born. How does any woman manage without a sister? I sometimes feel if our first baby had lived she would have made a difference to Stella. She could have confided in a sister earlier about her irritation with me and her rancour might not have grown into this hatred she feels for me now. She tells me that by making her keep the baby a secret from her brothers I have cut her off from them. But she never was close to Brian and David, and Patrick always loved her. He told me while she was away with you that he missed her because he loved her more than anybody in the world, more than me or his father. Now she takes no notice of him. Granted he's two years older and not a cuddly little boy any more, but he tells her jokes and she won't laugh and he asks her riddles and she doesn't answer. I feel like shaking her.

What should I have done when she told me she was pregnant? That's what I asked her this morning. I thought we were doing the best we could in saying she was taking a year away from the university to work in a bookshop in Oxford and live with you and Terence and give a hand with your children. I know there were raised eyebrows round here when she didn't come home for Christmas but I said, 'You know what they're like at that age – they do what they feel like at the moment.' After that I began to tell people we were planning to adopt a baby due to be born in March to a girl Stella had met in Oxford. I used to have to try and get Owen to stop looking so gloomy and bowed. It aged him ten years – it really did. I'd waken in the morning seeing blue skies and then I'd remember about Stella over with you, waiting for her baby without a husband to comfort her or me to mind her, and while I was washing my face I'd cry into the wash-basin and dry away the tears with the towel because I daren't let anybody see me in that state.

I don't want to boss people about or to control their lives, but I have never found anybody else prepared to make the decisions. I've been aware of my bossiness for a long time – since just before I left school. I never told anybody at home but I decided then that I had better be a nun. I was miserable at boarding-school, homesick from morning to night, hating the way every minute was in some timetable. That's why, after me, you were made to travel to school by bike and bus, getting soaked as often as not and constantly complaining about the activities you missed. The only time I was happy was in the Chapel. You remember the Chapel – all soaring white, and our September miseries ambered by the sun through the west window while we sang the Magnificat, our voices high and pure in the very controlled plain chant? Someone told me that my red hair under the black mantilla looked beautiful in that light. I treasured the compliment. I thought if I could stay there on my knees and say, 'Here I am, Lord,' he would reach down His hand and I would reach up mine (figuratively, of course) and I could reflect His beauty and order in a pool of sunshine all the rest of my life. So I went to Sister Ambrose and told her I was thinking of becoming a nun and she said, 'Now, Kathleen, you will have to give that serious thought. We'll leave it to God's will but I myself think you are quite unsuited to community life. You must realise you have not settled happily at all during the six years you have been with us.' I told her I knew that but I was prepared to offer that up and she said, oh very drily, 'I imagine it would be an uncomfortable position for the Sisters – being offered up. The truth is, Kathleen, that you never come into any group without directing them what to do and how to do it.' I just gasped a couple of times and went out of the room.

I had never noticed it in myself but I tried to stop it and more or less managed until I got married, but, my God, Peggy, if I didn't tell everybody what to do here they would all just drift. I keep wishing they had plans of their own, for jobs or holidays or anything. I keep hoping when they don't mention anything they have secret ideas, but no. At the last minute I am asked, 'What do *you* think I should do?' I didn't force Stella into the university. We repeatedly asked her what she wanted to do and she shrugged or muttered that she didn't know and took herself off to her room. I thought an arts degree would be no burden to her but we didn't make her do it – it costs us plenty. We promised ourselves never to mention how little we can afford it, although sometimes nowadays Owen begins to growl about it to Brian and David. When he catches my eye he stops. Isn't it a strange thing that she's passed every exam since then, only it doesn't seem to lift her heart at all? She sits her finals in a couple of months and then she'll be finished with study if she wants to be. There is nothing to prevent her getting a job, untrammelled, meeting people, living whatever kind of life she makes for herself. She says that by keeping Susan in the house I will never let her forget what she's been through. I don't know what to think.

Is she telling me the real truth in this version of Susan's conception or is she dressing up her weakness in the guise of decision, knowing how I laud decisiveness and deplore its lack? Or does she care what I approve of? She does hate me. She told me so and I know it to be true and I will find it difficult to live with. If the words had not been spoken I could have coped better. If she had only glared hatred I could have told myself she was in bad form or overworked, and that anyway she is not at her best in the mornings. But she put it into words and I'll not be able to forget it. Why did I show her the letter? It was an unfriendly act, I must confess, to shake her out of her frowsty yawns. She never used to sit around like this in the mornings. Did she do it in your house? When she came home I didn't like to say anything because I thought she needed extra consideration and gentleness. While I'm dressing and feeding Susan she sits there, shows no interest, doesn't smile when Susan chuckles or chatters. She blights our enjoyment of that part of the day. She tells me now that she hates the clothes I put on Susan, trousers or dungarees and jerseys, unchanged since she herself was that age. There are frilly old-world dresses she says would suit Susan beautifully and would show she belonged to a different generation. But Susan goes out to play with all the children on the road and she would not be comfortable or indeed warm enough in pretty dresses. She is the loveliest, happiest child, Peggy, mischievous and energetic. Stella says I make a fool of myself running after her, that I am too old and too stout and that if I'm going to bend over on the footpath to lift up a struggling child I should wear tights and not stockings. Oh she can mortify me with her tongue. I felt the same shame I used to feel on the hockey field when Sister Reginald used to shout, 'Spaces, Kathleen,' and it was nothing to do with the game but with a bit of leg escaped between black stockings and navy knickers.

I hope your children never wound you, Peggy. Yours are younger, of course, but, oh dear, do be careful never to make them your enemies. You have an advantage over me in that you are affectionate and demonstrative. Why are we so different, both reared the same way? I'd like to blame the boarding-school but I can't honestly believe that I would be any more prone to hugging and kissing if I had stayed at home. Once the children are as tall as I am I no longer touch them, nor they me. I love to look at them and listen to them and think about them, but I don't touch them. Patrick will soon be out of my reach. That's why Susan is such a bonus to me.

Do you remember when I went over to bring her home? I behaved very badly and you were mad with me. I've been sorry ever since but then I could act in no other way. All I could think of was to separate Stella from the baby so that nobody would connect them in their minds, your children, your Terence, your neighbours, even though they knew, they wouldn't think in the future of the baby being anything to do with Stella if I whisked her away quickly and left Stella behind until the end of the summer. Terence wanted to show me Oxford and I wish now I had seen it properly because when will I have the chance again? All I have is a confused impression of sulphur-coloured colleges in a murky mist of rain and boated bends of river swelling quietly in fields the way no Irish river ever did. I am glad your beautiful house stands on a hill. Next time I come I will be relaxed and enjoy your company and your affluence and I won't be always on my feet with anxiety to catch the plane. Stella says I never looked at her in the hospital and it could well be true. On the plane back with the little unknown baby on my knee I thought the best thing would be for the aeroplane to fall out of the sky, through the clouds, and we'd all be dead before we hit the ground. Rather, the baby and I would be dead, never mind the other passengers, and our troubles would be over, hers and mine and Stella's too. Then I remembered Patrick at home aged eight and I hadn't even a present for him. Sure enough, when I got out of the taxi there he was on his own because Brian and David had taken themselves off hostelling in Kerry as soon as I was gone and Owen had gone to work having asked Maura next door to keep an eye on him, that he'd be all right. He burst into tears when he saw me, he was so relieved, but for ages afterwards he kept on asking me what did I need a baby for. I think he has always resented losing his place as the youngest.

Owen complained about losing his sleep with a new baby wakening up in the night and he doesn't like having the cot in our room still. There is no bedroom for Susan and he suggests putting her in with Stella. I can't do that the way things are. I used to examine Susan for resemblances to Stella. I had my answer ready for any neighbour who would see some hint. I would point out that the butcher's wife adopted two little girls who grew not only to resemble her but each other. The only family sign I could see in Susan is the way her curls grow out in circles from the crown of her head exactly the same as the white waves on my mother-in-law. But she is old and living in Kilkenny and nobody else saw it, not even Owen, but he doesn't look at Susan the way he looked at his own. There's something a bit primitive about him that he balks at bringing up another man's child. But I love her. I love her tight warm little body. I love the bright intelligent way she has of looking at me as if I always know what she has in her mind. I never enjoyed my other children. At least that's the way it seems to me, looking back. They came too close together, except Patrick, and I was tired and bothered and haunted by the death of our first baby. That knocked all the confidence out of me. I stopped being young then. Only Owen has any idea. Now I think I could bear anything in the world so long as Susan is well and happy. I waken up in the night sometimes in terror that she'd get sick or be killed in an accident and I have to get up and look at her in her cot.

If Stella is unhappy living in this house she can move out to a flat once she's in a job and Susan can have her room. Or we can build an extension when we scrape up the money. It will be for Stella to choose. I will never refer again to her outburst of this morning. That's why I'm getting it off my chest to you. I don't expect you to make any answer to all of this. Don't worry. Everything is again under control.

I will write in a day or two an ordinary letter and ask about Terence, and your children in their international school and why your children and mine and those of my neighbours have always walked on walls and shouted on Sundays while English children never do. Are we such savages? Isn't it a pity you can't relax in a holiday at home, where they could run through fields and play in barns. But our own brother having got the place has no welcome for either of us. When I have time to think of it I resent that our families are condemned to concrete, cut off by him from where we were reared. That's an exaggeration; it's probably all an exaggeration – the whole letter.

Love

Kathleen

Heaven

Heaven

To Hilary in her sixties, heaven was an empty house. She loved to come in from shopping and shut the door behind her knowing that there was nobody in any of the seven neat rooms and that nobody would arrive home until her husband did, shortly after six. A daughter-in-law might wish to call on her for some service but she had insisted from the beginning that they telephone first to arrange a suitable time. She noticed sometimes her opposite neighbour being visited by people who turned the key in the door and walked in. That, to Hilary, would have been intolerable. Occasionally someone said to her that she must be lonely with her four sons grown and gone. She smiled and murmured something about keeping busy and anyway when her sons were healthy and happy that was all that mattered.

She had appeared always as a devoted mother. When she was young her pram had been polished, the pillow immaculate, the blankets fluffy, the baby perfect. The nappies on the line were white and square like a television advertisement. The standard in the district was high except for a few unfortunate backsliders but Hilary was out on her own. Her little boys playing with the other children got dirty in the normal way but it was obviously newly acquired dirt on clean clothes, not general grubbiness. She was fortunate perhaps in that they all had her blonde pink-and-white appearance. None of them had inherited their father's dark hair and shadowed skin although they were tall like him and thin. Hilary often said then that she should slim but instead she dressed in drifty floaty clothes, and before hats went out of fashion she wore black gauzy hats with red cherries, or pink hats with veils or green hats with roses. She dressed up every afternoon to wheel out the pram and do the shopping. Some of the neighbours admired her style, and others criticised that but admitted she had great spirit.

The effort of all this perfectionism drained her each day so that when the children were eventually in bed she sat down by the fire and her husband sat in the opposite chair. She glanced at magazines and ate sweets and sighed or yawned every now and again. He read the papers in their entirety and switched the television from snowy channel to foggy channel and back so that it blared all evening until it closed down for the night. At least then the noise came from one place only. Later, when the boys were in their teens, Hilary had to tolerate transistors in bedrooms and tape recorders as well as the television and record player. So long as she stayed in her kitchen she had some slight refuge but it was there that the younger boys brought their troubles with sums, or spellings to hear or Irish passages to learn, while the older ones brought their complaints about unfair teachers or biased referees.

These worried her. It upset her to see their soft curved mouths drawn down in ugly resentment. She tried to persuade them not to feel aggrieved so readily, that it would become a habit and give them indigestion. She had to laugh them out of it because they would have been very embarrassed if she had confessed that she feared the harm it would do their souls. She never said such things to anyone. The only time she spoke out was at a parents' meeting once in the boys' school. There had been an alarming increase in rugby injuries to boys' spines, not in the school but in the country generally, news of brilliant boys paralysed for life. Some of the parents asked the priests who ran the school how their boys were safeguarded. The priests marshalled reassurances and the parents failed to put forward sensible objections. Hilary said she thought rugby an uncivilised game anyway, and the rivalry between schools concerning rugby and between the priests involved was completely unchristian. There was a murmur of dissent and then several men shouted no, no.

'If anything happens to any of my boys on the rugby field,' Hilary persisted, 'I will go and howl outside the priests' house day and night.'

The other parents laughed but Hilary did not laugh and the priests did not really laugh either and none of her boys made much progress at rugby from that time on.

They did well at everything else, though, much better in their exams than their teachers ever expected going by their class marks and by their judgements to Hilary during parent–teacher meetings. They went to university and there followed years of counting every penny to keep them there, of going without new clothes, of wearing cheap shoes long after they were broken and spread. Her husband had to keep his old car when it was a daily torment of refusing to start in the mornings or even at traffic lights, and people pushing it and looking as if they might get heart attacks. But they did well so that their father often wondered aloud how far he too might have gone in this world if he had had the chances they were getting. Hilary never had such thoughts about herself. She fed them nourishing food morning and night, worried about their not having enough sleep, listened to their panic about exams, and to relieve the terrible feelings of impotence she had about them began going to Mass every morning to pray for their success. Then they were all finished, all with jobs except the youngest who was awarded a grant to do a Ph.D in an American university and insisted on marrying before he went, to his father's disgust. He fumed and fussed and denounced it as lunatic but Hilary was relieved because she had read novels about American universities and she could hardly believe such depravity existed. A wife would keep him safe.

Even before the others married she found herself alone in the house for long hours during the day. At first she would stand in the hall with her hands clasped, looking into empty rooms and wondering how she would celebrate. She generally finished up making herself tea and cake or eating a bar of chocolate with a feeling that there was something she was missing. Gradually she realised that this was not an occasional luxury, this solitude, but a routine. So she fixed a time every morning to sit and relish the quiet. As the days passed she grew more intense about it so that frequently the blood surged in her ears and she was whirled into a great cone of silence and stayed there suspended. She had no thoughts, no contemplations. She was not aware of the happiness it induced until she resumed her household activities and found herself smiling. She began hurrying home in the mornings to shut herself in. Only years of discipline insisted that she cleaned, washed and cooked as she always did. Sometimes the silence caught her up out of doors so that she drifted past people without seeing them or speaking to them.

She began thinking of heaven. She imagined deep silence. Innumerable people stood in rapture, no one touching another, backed and divided by pillars and arches as in Renaissance paintings, drawn, she supposed, to God whom she could not imagine, but still and complete in themselves. She was confident she was going there, seeing herself as a middle-aged to elderly ewe in the middle of the flock giving no trouble at all to the shepherd. She had never had any great temptations; she was unlikely, she thought, to have any now. At funeral Masses she happily saw herself as the dead person and arranged in her mind how things should be done about food, flowers and cars. No one would miss her, she had done all that had been asked of her, she could fade out any time.

She did do baby-sitting for the grandchildren whenever she was asked, until her eldest son took his wife off for a holiday to celebrate her getting a job and left their three-year-old boy with Hilary for a fortnight. By the end of the first week she was consumed by the same desire for perfection in everything to do with this grandson as with her sons more than twenty years before. His hair must shine, his teeth must gleam, his clothes must grace his little straight sturdy body. When she watched him concentrating on a toy she contemplated the possibility of his being lonely at any time in the future or unhappy or unsuccessful and could hardly bear the pain. When her son came to collect him he congratulated her on the child's fine appearance.

'It'll be all right to leave him round on Monday morning when Pauline and I are going to work, won't it?' he asked casually, and Hilary said, 'No, not at all,' sharply, and then made excuses that she was too old, that he'd be better in his own home with someone in to look after him. 'We don't know anybody suitable,' her son protested. 'It's risky to let in someone we don't know. She might not care for him properly.'

'He is your child,' she said tartly. 'He is your responsibility, yours and Pauline's. You cannot shift it on to me. You'll just have to pay somebody well and hope for the best.'

He seized on that. 'But we have every intention of paying you. Of course we had. You mustn't think . . .'

'How much would you have thought of? Five pounds a

week? No, no, no, money wouldn't make any difference.'

They had actually thought that if there were any question of money they should offer twenty pounds a month – it would be better paid by the month – but that indeed it was unlikely she would take any money. What would she want money for? She never bought anything except just the necessary food. She would be so glad of the child's company during her long empty day. He would give her a fresh interest in life and they'd pick him up most evenings after work.

They did not forgive her. The child was left in a playschool in the mornings and collected by a neighbour who minded him with her own children until his parents came home. It was not satisfactory, really. Hilary, after a week or two of sleepless nights, managed to put him out of her mind most of the time. A year later, tidying a drawer, she came across a silly affectionate birthday card given to her by one of her sons when he was young and felt a pang. It was nice after all when she was of use to them so that they loved her.

One morning her husband opened a letter that made him laugh first and then angered him.

'What is it?' she said with only a polite interest. He hesitated for a minute and then handed it over. It said:

Dear Sir,

You should know your wife is an alcoholic. She is being talked about all over the district. She hurries home in the mornings without talking to her neighbours and shuts herself in the house. Some of these days she will disgrace you.

Signed
A Wellwisher

She was alarmed, even though the letter-writer had mistaken the object of her addiction.

'I shouldn't have shown it to you,' he said, looking at her in surprise. 'It's upset you. Sure we all know you drink nothing but coffee and tea, although you drink plenty of them. It's only some crank.' He was watching her, though, and when he came home from work he continued to watch her. He suggested they go for a walk. She refused, murmuring something about tired feet. The next night he thought they should go for a drive. She hadn't been in the car for years except for Sunday Mass or Friday-night shopping.

'What would we do that for?' she asked, embarrassed. 'It's threatening rain.' The attention unnerved her, making it more difficult for her to escape into silence, but she could cope so long as he was there only in the evening.

Then he retired. She had known for years the date of his retirement but refused to face it, as did he.

He would give full attention to the garden, he said, and he tramped in and out of her kitchen, needing water when she was at the sink, wanting her hand to hold a line for beds he was digging. He grunted and groaned and held his hand to the small of his long back. He didn't enjoy it. He had no company. His dark face grew more and more saturnine. Hilary dreaded coming home to him. He had stopped watching her but he continued the recent invitations to walks, drives, meals out. They were no longer a lifeline for her but for himself. She refused, regardless. She had always an excuse; she was tired, she had no clothes. She had never revived her interest in clothes, suppressed while the money was needed for her growing family. She wore black trousers with an elastic waistband and any kind of tunic on top. He urged her to buy something else but she put it off.

One rainy day, when he was sitting in the kitchen rubbing

continuously at the threadbare places on the knees of his trousers, he asked, 'Hilary, why did you marry me?'

'Such a thing to ask, out of the blue,' she said, taken aback. 'Have you nothing better to think about than ancient history?'

'It's not ancient history. Whatever there was then surely keeps on now. You don't love me now; you can't stand me around the place. Did you love me ever, that's what I want to know? That's what I have to know.'

'For goodness' sake, it's just that I'm not used to somebody under my feet in the daytime. You're miserable yourself – you should think of something to get you out among other men.'

'You're not answering me.' He kept on so that she snapped at him, 'And I'm not going to answer you. How can I remember what it was like when I was young?'

He said no more but sat there, hunched.

She was uncomfortable, remembering clearly what it was like to see her twenties speeding by, and in spite of her blonde hair and pink cheeks and Ballybunion and Salthill and Tramore and numerous escorts nobody had offered to marry her. She had seized on the prospect of marriage with him as the only way to a real life – her old life had no sense or meaning. They had been well suited, neither until now interested in the other. She had had her children, her house and then her silence. He had had his job and his children to a certain extent. Now he had nothing and, she thought indignantly, he was busy seeing that she'd have nothing either.

While he was about the house she never sat down until night-time. She polished and cleaned things that were already shining. She hovered over the cooker as it cooked their simple meals. He was either in the kitchen reading his paper or in and out of the garden. His breathing banished silence from the house. The smallest sounds impinged on her – the gentle bong of a Venetian blind upstairs at an open window, the click of a thermostat in the bathroom as it turned itself on or off, the ticking of clocks all over the house, unsynchronised.

Before the winter set in she told the priest at her monthly Confession, 'I have feelings of hatred for my husband, murderous feelings. I am afraid I will do him an injury – I have carving knives and heavy casseroles in the kitchen.' The priest told her to pray about it, to see a doctor, to get a hobby for herself or her husband. 'But,' he warned her, 'don't let hatred enter into your soul or you'll be fighting it until your dying day.' She was afraid then of losing her peace in heaven as well as the peace in her home. All the beautiful broad shining avenues of silence would be shut off from her and she would be condemned to some shrieking cacophonous pit.

She urged the buying of a garden shed and a greenhouse to occupy him. He was not enthusiastic about them but he consented after long deliberations on the back mat over where they were to go and then what was to go in them. She tried putting a chair in the shed and bringing out his morning coffee and afternoon tea, but she could not put him out of her mind. Every time she glanced out of the window she could see his shape, stooped. She could even see the sun sparkling on the drip at the end of his nose.

She resigned herself and rang up her daughters-in-law. 'I will mind your children after playschool,' she told them. 'I need my mornings for messages and housework but I'll have them on a regular basis from lunchtime until you come home from work. I don't want any money for it. Their grandfather can collect them. He'll help me with them. I'll not find them too much for me while he is there.'

They were stiff. They were dubious. 'You would need to be sure you're not just using our children to cover your own loneliness,' Pauline said.

'I have never been lonely, Pauline, never in my life,' she answered mildly, so they allowed themselves to be persuaded and every afternoon five children aged between two and six invaded her life.

She had one of her sons go up to the roof-space and bring down all the toys and books stored there since his own childhood, and because there were no girls' playthings she produced her old green and rose-petalled hats so they could dress up. She put a load of builders' sand in the back garden and saw it tramped everywhere. She was vigilant that they didn't rub it into one another's eyes or use the spades as weapons. She hugged them when they cried and loved their hot damp foreheads pressing into her neck. After their tea she sorted them out from the debris, packed them into the car and her husband delivered them to their three separate homes. Apart from collecting and delivering the children he took no interest in them. When the elder son of his eldest son put his hand on his knee and said, 'Come on out and kick football, Grandfather,' he almost blushed but made an excuse and went up to the bathroom, no refuge with five children in the house. One evening he told her that he was tired of the arrangement, too old to suffer all those children. He would still act as chauffeur but he had met another grandfather at the playschool and they had decided to go to a bowling-green not far away on good afternoons and to a quiet pub if it rained. He would not be at home at that time for the foreseeable future. There were plenty of things to do for a retired man still active and alert. Hilary agreed, told him he was perfectly right, and sat down exhausted every evening when she had cleaned up the mess left by the children, far too tired to do anything but leaf through a magazine or glance now and then at her husband's choice of television programmes, six clear channels now, one always blaring.

HEAVEN

Now and again, though, she did catch a distant glimpse of calm corridors and vaulted roofs all soundless and it gave her a feeling of great sweetness in anticipation.

A Literary Woman

A Literary Woman

When I saw the ad in the evening paper I thought, 'That's for me.' If I buy the paper I read all the ads, lost and found, articles for sale, column after column. There was a time when I had to read the situations vacant, and I will again fairly soon, but then I had enough money to go on with. 'Furnished apartment in private house, to let. Bed-sit, kitchenette and bathroom' and a telephone number. That was the advertisement.

I have my own flat. I've had it for forty years in my own name since my mother died when I was fifteen. I'm sure it wasn't legal then but nobody ever tried to put me out. I've come back here after every job finished, after every old lady died that I was looking after. At first I am pleased about being in my own place. Then I get discontented. It is dark. It's overlooked by other big sooty blocks. The old ladies lived in substantial houses with big rooms and gardens, well away from the city centre. I enjoyed living in those houses even though a great many of them were falling to bits because there was nobody to look after them, any more than to look after their occupants. I was able to keep myself comfortable enough by spending their money on coal and oil and electricity. I wasn't going to economise for them. Piles of money they all had, salted away. I got my hands on some of it, legally. I was very careful about the law. That was why I wasn't in a job when I rang the number in the advertisement.

The next morning I followed the directions the woman gave me on the phone. When I got off the bus I saw there was no old money in these houses. Three-bedroom or four-bedroom semi-detached except for one empty all by itself at the end of the road. They were prim and respectable. The hedges were all cut, the grass all trimmed, the curtains all straight, but nothing to admire except neatness, if you like neatness. It was eleven o'clock in the morning but the whole place was silent as the grave, not a soul stirring. The house I arrived at had built on over the garage. I could see the join. I thought the extension might sag some day, but not while I was in it. I wouldn't stay very long.

A big woman opened the door and her smile wavered when she saw me. I'm a big woman too but there was a difference. She was taller, with a big bust and hips and in tight at the waist. I'm just broad all over. A fine-looking woman, they'd have said about her down the country – a high colour in her cheeks, dark hair going grey. I don't like women with rosy cheeks. I'm always pale. My mother was pale. She died of anaemia.

'I'm Miss Teeling,' I said. 'I rang you yesterday about the flat to let.' There was a warm smell coming out of the house. I could see down the hall, a meagre hall, through the end of the kitchen out to the back garden. It was sunny with trees. Maybe it reminded me of the country, although I don't have any good memories of the country. I don't have good memories of any place.

'Oh. I wasn't expecting someone like you,' she said. 'I was expecting someone young.' I knew that. I had made my voice light and timid on the phone. I just stood there, looking at her. She gave in. 'Well you'd better have a cup of tea after your bus journey.' I followed her into the kitchen and I saw then why I had thought of the country. The warm smell was from the range. It was white with a shiny black top, not like the all-black models my mother used to have to black-lead and keep stoked, no matter what the weather was like. Here, there was a griddle pulled over to the side with triangular scones standing on one end and little bits of flour turning brown. She didn't give me any of them with my tea. She got out a Yellow Pack of fig rolls and offered me one. I didn't take it. I sipped my tea and left her to do the talking. I knew she felt awkward.

'I was thinking of a student or a young girl away from home, working in the civil service maybe, without a lot of money to pay rent. I had six children myself and they are reared now, and married in Dublin. They don't even have to stay here overnight. I thought it would be nice to have somebody young about the place again. Of course my family visit and bring their children. I'm not lonely. But I didn't think it right to have accommodation going to waste.' She would have gone on for ever.

'I thought yesterday when I saw your advertisement that the Sacred Heart had picked out some place for me to live,' I said. I had noticed the holy-water font in the hall with the sprig of palm over it, and a picture of the Blessed Virgin saying her prayers above the fireplace. 'I have great faith in the Sacred Heart,' I went on. 'I have a flat of my own in the inner city,' I told her. 'But it's not a bit nice. I keep my part nice, but the stairs are concrete public stairs and I'm always in terror somebody will attack me going up or down. The things that go on on those stairs you'd never believe – drink and drugs, and worse. It's hard on a respectable woman. I'm promised one of the new little houses for single people like me. It won't

be long before I get into it. In the meantime I thought I'd
enjoy the good healthy living out here. People like you who
have always had good houses in nice surroundings don't know
what it's like for people like me.'

I got out this pathetic-looking bundle of references and gave
them over to her. Some of them were ages old. Some of
them I'd written myself. One was from a priest that I'd been
housekeeper for, twenty years ago. I lasted three weeks until
his mother came to visit and told him to get rid of me because
Satan was in me. I would not have corrupted him. I never
wanted any man to touch me. I never wanted anybody to touch
me, as far back as I can remember. Out loud in front of me
she said it. So he did what he was told, only he wrote me a
great reference. He wrote how unfortunate I'd been, left an
orphan at fifteen, always worked hard, attended to my religious
duties, deserved a chance. It was very useful to me down the
years, a priest's reference. But this woman never looked at
them, just fingered them a bit.

'The bus service is not good at all,' she said. 'It would be
awkward for you getting to your work.' She was trying hard
but I knew she was going to give in. I can't stand people who
let me bully them. All those old women I'd begin to work for
with a bit of respect. I could see them surrounded by good
solid furniture even if it was covered with dust as often as not.
By the time I was with them a couple of months they'd be
begging me to do this or that for them, things they were
beyond doing for themselves, and I'd despise them in my
heart. At least they were old or incapable. There was no excuse
for this Maeve O'Reilly. She could have told me to go, but
she didn't.

'Oh I don't work just now,' I said. 'A grateful patient of
mine left me some money and the doctor told me I was in need
of rest and fresh air.'

'I couldn't possibly have somebody here all day,' she said, somewhat like a gasping fish.

'Could I have a look at the rooms?' I asked. 'I could be thinking of them and imagining how pleasant it would have been, while I'm in my dark flat. There's a smell of gas there a lot of the time.'

She led me up the stairs, me puffing and panting to let her know how delicate I was. She turned left at the landing into a little corridor with a narrow window at the end of it. On the window-ledge for some reason sat a big white stone. On the left was a fair-sized room, the bed-sittingroom, with a window over the street. On the other side was a bathroom and a slice of a room made into the most orderly kitchen you ever saw. It looked out over the garden. Tulips were open, beginning to fall, and apple blossom thinking of coming out, a suggestion of pink. I turned back into the sitting-room. That was not a good name for it; I had to stand to see from the window what was going on in the road. I pointed this out to Madam Maeve O'Reilly to let her know it wasn't all perfection. She explained that they had had to do that to keep the windows at an even height outside when they built the extension. I was going to tell her that when the extension sagged they would not be level anyway but I thought that would do for later.

'I'll give you a month's rent now,' I said. 'At the end of that time, if you don't like me or I don't like you, we can review the situation.' How often had I had the last bit said to me when I was taken on for a job. They never got rid of me and I didn't think Madam would get rid of me here either. She sighed and said, 'Well – ' and took the money.

I went back to my own flat. It was up concrete steps but there was nothing wrong with the people who used them and I never was afraid of anybody there. I often thought the young people there were afraid of me. I heard a boy once telling his friends that I was a witch. They'd stand back to let me pass as if I was the queen. While I was living in old women's houses nobody ever squatted in my flat. Nobody ever broke in.

That night I had letters to burn. All the time I was working for people I had written letters telling them what I thought of them. While I was being pleasant and submissive in the face of their sour temper I was writing screeds telling them what I really thought of the smells in their houses, of their false teeth gone rattly, of their falling hair or hairy chins, of their incontinence. I never posted them. How could I? They might have discovered I had written them, and then I'd be out of a job, maybe for good.

Of course the only jobs I took were where I was in charge. I didn't want family members telling me what to do or not do. At least, they could tell me what they liked so long as they took themselves off to their own houses afterwards, and they were ready enough to go, leaving me to look after things in my own way. I was capable and efficient when I wanted to be, when doctors were visiting or when I had got what I wanted. It was money I wanted. It was money I got. My last patient, Mrs O'Malley, was a solicitor's widow with no family. She could not get out of bed without my help. She could ring her bell, she could bang her black stick, she could call till her voice failed. But if I stayed downstairs drinking my tea and reading my library book what could she do? Her doctor thought she was rambling. Her nephew didn't want to be bothered. Once she put me in her will I nursed her perfectly, aired sheets, fresh nightdresses, clean hair, spotless bedroom. She hated me. I got great satisfaction from seeing how she hated me – in her big house with all her money and her fine accent, reduced to hating me.

'You'll die alone, Miss Teeling,' she told me.

'We all die alone, Mrs O'Malley,' I told her. 'I'll be better equipped for it than most.'

'God knows all of this,' she said. 'I hope He forgives you.'

That really made me laugh. I'd been reared on that in every school I went to. God knows all things. God loves. God forgives. God is all-powerful. But I gloated over my knowledge that He can't prevent the consequences of what we do. I tormented and deprived old Mrs O'Malley until I was left money in her will. She wasn't the only one either. God could keep Mrs O'Malley alive for a long time, and indeed He did, but she had to die sometime, and no power in heaven or on earth could stop me inheriting the money. The value had gone down somewhat, it is true. I believe in God. Only a fool wouldn't believe in God. So many nasty things could not happen accidentally. He knows all things so that He will know the tenderest place to aim the blow. I've seen it. Women who enjoyed talking end up mumbling or lose the power of speech. Women who were proud of their figures develop into bent-backed crones. Oh He is mighty and He can do great things but I am an independent operator. I can compete in my own small way.

I brought my suitcase the next evening to the O'Reillys' house and the husband carried it up the stairs for me. A big middle-aged man, he did not lift his eyes until I said thanks and then I could see how little he liked the thought of me, or the look of me. They gave me a front-door key, thinking they wouldn't notice me much, but I coughed and gasped up and down the stairs and hovered on the landing, clearing my throat, so that they could never think they were alone in the house. He was some kind of traveller; he was away often enough in the middle of the week. Her sons and daughters came to visit with their families. I never bothered to work out who was who, or what belonged to which. She minded children for young women around and she had neighbours coming in at all hours and staying for long sessions. The man next door came in each night her husband was away to check that she was all right. He was in and out in a minute unless she wanted him to fix something. Maeve and Kevin they were to each other. I haven't been anything but Miss Teeling for years and years.

The days were endless. I was making the O'Reillys uncomfortable but I wasn't doing any good to myself. My stomach kept on giving me trouble. Every time I was bored I'd go into the little model kitchen to make myself tea. I'd debate with myself if I should have something to eat with it. I don't like a cup of tea by itself. I'd eat a biscuit or a slice of bread and I'd be sorry. It was no wonder I was so fat.

I watched big drops of rain falling in a kind of bird-bath arrangement they had in the back garden. I remembered one day at a school in the country. We were told to do a composition on rain because it was a wet day and the teacher was too lazy to think of anything else. The sky was dark and streams of rain were running down the tall dirty windows. I wrote, 'It is pouring rain.' Then I stopped. The teacher came round. 'Come along, Winifred. You've got the gift of the gab. And with your mother being a teacher once, you should know how to use it.' She put her hand on my shoulder and I thought to myself, 'What right has she to touch me when she is telling lies about my mother who certainly is no teacher?' So I didn't write another word and then it was a changed tune. 'Ugly big girl, idling your time and mine,' she shouted while she shook me and thumped my back. I was big all right. And why was I big? Because every time I changed schools they put me back a class. 'What class were you in when you lived in Carlow? Third class? Well we'll try you in second.' I went back to the farmers' house where my mother was a servant – maid-of-all-work or housekeeper, whatever way you want to look at it. They were two middle-aged bachelor brothers and she cleaned and cooked for them. She and I slept in a bedroom over the kitchen, under the roof. She made me stay up there any time they were about the house. I got into the way early of hiding in other people's houses. When I was smaller I'd want to stay near the fire or watch my mother baking but if the men came in I was banished to our quarters. 'Leave her alone,' they would say in the beginning. 'What harm is the child doing?' She paid them no heed. That day I told her about the teacher's mistake and in less than a week we were gone to a new school and a new job in another part of the country.

We never settled, until we got the flat in Dublin after I was finished my schooling, all the bits of it that I ever got. The only reason we didn't move from there was that she got too sick. And then she died.

When I stood at the front window looking at these warm comfortable houses with families living there for years, I told myself how dull it was. It certainly was dull for me, watching. The only time there was any movement in the road was when the children were going to or from school. There were not many children living in the road, only a handful really. But they came down from other avenues and drives and parks – all the same kind of people from the same smug houses. Parents and minders of various ages brought them to the school, holding hands, talking to them, laughing with them, beaming down at them. I never liked children, never took a job where I might meet children. They stare at you and then say something cheeky. But I began to go out at that time to the shops beside the school and again when school closed for the day and the children were met. I was taken aback at the way those young women used the name of God. Second, thou shalt not take the name of the Lord thy God in vain. I'd learnt that in school often enough. I admired the sound of it. But they didn't know it. I listened to the gossip although it took me a while to work it out because I knew nobody.

One bit was clear enough. Remarks were made about the newly appointed head teacher, that it was strange he'd never married, though somebody said she thought he was engaged. They laughed that he'd been very attentive to his mother but that she'd been dead for a few years now. Two of them sniggered that he was very good with the boys. Others looked disapproving and whooshed their children out of earshot. It was easy to pick up his name and the phone book gave me his address. I bought a writing-pad and envelopes.

Dear Mr Corrigan,

It is well known that you are homosexual. The parents are talking about you. Somebody will go to the priests and you will lose your job. Boys are not safe with you. The only thing you can do is get married.

> Signed
> A Wellwisher

I wrote that. It was different from the way I used to do the letters to my employers – they were pages long. I kept it in my handbag for nearly a week before posting. I only wanted a bit of excitement, something to happen. Of course nothing happened. I saw him putting the children into a bus the next week.

'Good morning, Mr Corrigan,' a woman said to him. He was a tall thin man with dark-red hair, very composed and good-humoured, not a bit put out by my letter. He lived in a bungalow on the road behind the O'Reillys' house. I hadn't actually seen the letter delivered so I thought maybe he never got it. I decided to keep my letters for the road I could look out on.

There was a scratty little boy in the house opposite. I saw him lifting a bar of chocolate in the shop. He was well dressed with good shoes and anorak and clean, well-pressed jeans so that he had no excuse for stealing chocolate. He let himself into an empty house every day after school. Sometimes he sat outside on the step. He looked miserable at times, a bit like I used to feel when I was going to school in one strange place after another. He was thin, though, and I was fat. In one place the children got it into their heads that I belonged to the tinkers and they chased me, yelling at me. I suppose it was because of the clothes I wore, all hand-outs from people whose children had grown out of them, none of them bought for me.

I remember one time walking along in a Dublin park, holding my mother's hand. I had on a red coat with brass buttons, given to me by one charitable lady, and it had gone too short for me. Underneath I had a red skirt from another charitable lady. It was two inches longer and a different shade of red. I was mortified, thinking everybody in the park must be aware of my clashing colours. We had bread to give to the ducks and I threw it, calling to the ducks, but they took no notice because the water was littered with bread. They were overfed. Some rich children there with their father pushed against me, and if my mother had not been holding my hand I would have fallen into the green scummy water. They noticed me no more than the ducks did. My mother got a big stone in her two hands and heaved it into the pond so that the ducks and the people scattered squawking. She took my hand again and we walked away. We were splashed too, of course, but we didn't matter.

I wrote to the scratty boy's mother, telling her he was a shoplifter. I saw it in the postman's hand, pushing it through the letterbox, but I never knew what happened after that. The next morning I saw the mother and father drive off to work and later on the boy went out to school, testing the door to make sure he'd shut it safely. I didn't give up. There was a Belfast woman on the road – I hate their accent. I wrote to her warning her that she'd be shot. There is far too much attention paid to Belfast. There was another woman with a new baby. I wrote to her that her husband had had an affair while she was pregnant. I had never seen the man but she was far from beautiful.

One advantage God has over me – He knows what is happening. When He knocks people down He knows if they lie on the ground or scramble to their feet. He can watch them grovel, or hit them a kick if they don't. I cast my letters in the postbox and that was an end of it as far as I could see. I always want things to happen. Nothing happens. I'd have been better writing the big long letters that went nowhere but got all my feelings off my chest. How I hated those sick old women. I did not hate these people I wrote to. I knew very little about them. They had too good a life, that's all. Some of them were smug. They all had houses and families. When I get my own little house, I'll have no more need to write letters of any sort. In the meantime I walked to the library to change my books. I read hundreds of books. And I took buses to post my letters in different parts of the town. I was not stupid. I was never stupid although some teachers were confused about that.

It was a hot summer. I sweltered up there. Nobody ever told me I could go out to the garden. I didn't want to risk annoying Madam too much so I didn't go. I had sniffed the perfume of the apple blossom when it blew in my narrow window and I liked the shapes of the shadows the trees traced on the grass. She pulled the weeds out of the raspberry bushes one afternoon and I wished I could have done that, letting the sun shine in on all the canes. I never had a garden. Of course I could have worked in the old ladies' gardens but I wasn't going to do that. I was not paid to do that. I wondered sometimes if God was ever sorry He'd gone any further than creating the sun and the sky and the plants.

The sun shone into my slice of a kitchen. I stood at the window listening to her talking to her neighbours over the wall on either side. She'd feel me there and glance up, to see me parboiled. They talked about their children, how well they were getting on. Some of them were in Australia or Japan or America. All were doing great. The O'Reillys were in Dublin. She was constantly thanking God they were all in Dublin, all in jobs, all married, some of them with children. Sometimes she left the house empty and went off with them to the sea for the day. I hunted then through every room to see was there anything secret. She never locked doors against me. But I wasted my time. They were a dull pair. She greeted me when she met me, but politely, not pleasantly. He kept his head down. I'd hear him around the house singing her name to some tune, at the top of his voice. Then he'd remember about me, and break off.

In September she gave me a bagful of cooking apples. I meant to cook them because I don't eat enough fruit and vegetables. But when I quartered the first one a mealy-coloured grub nodded out at me. It gave my stomach a turn and when I met the same thing in two or three more I put them all out in her bin so that she'd see them. I was supposed to tie up my own rubbish in a plastic bag and leave it at the front gate on bin day but I wanted her to see what I thought of her gift. I wondered now and again if I really was a witch to put such a curse on the apples that had looked smooth and green and whole. I couldn't think of eating an apple for a while after that.

When the evenings closed in I thought where was the sense in my staying on. I told her I was going back early to my flat for Christmas to prepare for my relations who wanted to visit me there. Her face lit up, she was so glad to see me go. I said I'd be back after Christmas and I'd just take with me what belongings I needed. If she had ordered me to go, if she'd said she needed the rooms for somebody else, I'd have been happy enough to wipe the dust of the whole place off my feet. But she stood there and then she said, 'Maybe your new house will be ready by then,' and I answered, 'Oh not a chance of it.'

I haven't any relations. Maybe I have cousins some place but I don't know them, nor do I want to know them, and they don't know me and are lucky, I suppose, in that. I was not illegitimate. My mother insisted on that. It's a mystery to me why she cared, since I can't remember ever seeing my father. His name was on my birth certificate, Maurice Teeling, and my mother's maiden name, Kathleen Kelly. Nothing exotic about Kathleen Kelly and, besides, I knew her. She did her best for me as far as she could except in not getting her health seen to. But Maurice Teeling could be somebody. I read books, when I was young, where orphans found their true fathers who brought them home to servants and carpets ankle-deep. My mother would answer no questions about him, who he was, where he was. 'He is your father. We were married. I'll not speak ill of him.' It must have been fear of him that sent her tearing all over the country. Where were her parents or his parents? Nobody wanted us. She was all I had. I was all she had. I suppose I loved her. She looked after me but she was not a very loving mother. She was too harassed. I remember her hurrying in front of me, rushing, either pulling me along by the hand or calling over her shoulder to me, lagging, that we must make haste.

When we came to this flat I thought maybe we'd stopped running away. When my mother took to lying down on the sofa I thought it was that she was relaxed, being in her own domain. I thought maybe she'd heard that Maurice Teeling was dead. I got a job in a vegetable shop. I was cold all the time and my hands were black, with hacks. My mother had a cleaning job but one day she said she was too tired to go to work. Then she was too tired to get back upstairs so she didn't risk going down. I did the messages. Her face went the colour of bone. She lay on the green sofa under the window for weeks, eyes closed. I couldn't coax her to eat or to speak. At the end she just stayed in bed. I begged her to get up, to tell me what to do, to send me for the doctor. At the inquest the coroner said there had been no need whatever for her to die, that there was a simple way of keeping anaemia in check, that she could have lived until she was ninety.

I am surprised every year with the pleasure I get from the first warmth of the spring sun on the back of my head. It is different from the sun on my face and it is different from the sun later on in the year. It feels affectionate. It happens in February if I'm lucky. When I felt it outside St Patrick's Cathedral, surrounded by stone, brick and concrete, I made up my mind to go back to O'Reillys' house to relish the fresh air and the greenery.

When I turned my key in her lock and opened her front door and she looked out of the kitchen with such dismay, I made up my mind that she was the one to annoy with letters. I would see the effect then. She was the kind to take them to heart, I thought. The trouble was, there was nothing to taunt her with. So I sent her a Valentine card from the man next door. The rudeness of the card offended me so I knew it would offend her too. I saw it in the postman's hand, coming in the gate. I heard her go to the door and lift the letters. Almost immediately she departed for Mass and I slipped down to see what had happened to the card. There was no sign of it. Her husband came home in the evening with a bunch of flowers for her and I listened at the top of the stairs but I could hear no mention of the card.

I waited a few days and then I sat down to write her a love letter from the neighbour. I found it very difficult. I never knew any man. Except for those farmers whose houses we roosted in, I never lived in the same place as a man. No man ever touched me except for the odd shove from a master in school. All I could write were romantic bits out of books. They made me feel sick. I hoped they would make her feel sick too.

I began to go to Mass on weekdays to keep an eye on her and see would she confide in some of the other middle-aged women she met there. I never heard a single bit of gossip from them. They smiled at one another. They held doors, they stood back to let one another pass. The word that came into my head for them was 'gentle'. But they were nervous, timorous. They locked all their doors. They were afraid. I couldn't get over it. They had solid, staid houses in a quiet area and they felt threatened.

I sat in the same seat in the church every day. It was behind a pillar so that I would not see the altar. Other people shifted round so that the pillars didn't block their view. It was a big showy church. Beside it was an old oak tree. On windy autumn days the porch would be full of withered oak leaves, blown in. It was still bare the March day Maeve O'Reilly looked over at me from her seat on the opposite side of the church. She looked straight at me and I could see coming into her eyes the realisation that I had written the letters. I had wanted something to happen but I didn't feel too good just then. I left the church before anybody else and I was back in my room before she came home.

That afternoon I was standing at my window when a car stopped outside with two big men in it. The driver sat on and the other came up to the door. They were in plain clothes but anybody would have known they were guards. She brought him into the sitting-room and shut the door so that I could not hear a word. Her radio was still talking away in the kitchen. Then I heard them on the stairs and my mouth went dry. For a second I knew how my mother must have felt each time she took flight. I opened the door when it was knocked and there was an overweight youngish man with my letters wrapped up in cellophane. I could see the one to Maeve O'Reilly on top and a couple of others, two or three, I couldn't be sure.

'We have reason to believe you wrote these scurrilous letters,' he said in a strong country accent.

I didn't answer.

'What sense was there in annoying good decent people?' he asked. 'Didn't you know it was against the law to do such a thing?'

'It is not against the law if there is no threat,' I said to myself, because, as I said before, I am not stupid. But I could not make the words come out.

'I don't really want to prosecute,' she said from behind him. I was supposed to be grateful. 'If she would just go back to her own place.'

'We'll take you,' said the guard. 'Just pack up your things, Ma'am, and give Mrs O'Reilly here her keys. You'll have to stay away from this district in the future. We'd hear about it down at the station if you torment these people again.'

He stood there, awkward, while I padded in and out of the kitchen and bathroom, not hurrying myself, gathering my belongings. After a while she said to him maybe he'd like a cup of tea and he said, 'Oh no, not at all,' but he turned away and then he said, 'I'll carry your case for you when you're ready, Ma'am. Mrs O'Reilly will give me a shout.' He went and sat in the car. They had the windows rolled down because the sun was shining.

I sat in the back. They didn't seem to think I was very dangerous or one would have come in to guard me. Their coats were on the seat beside me. At the end of the road the car drove past the detached house that I had heard was haunted. It was empty again. That gave me some satisfaction when I thought of the arrogant young pair with their two cars.

I could not write any more letters. I realised that. Now that the police knew about me I would be caught and that would tell against me when I was due for my own little house. I saw the foolishness of all those fruitless letters. I had always been so keen on my notions that nobody and nothing could prevent consequences. Maybe God wasn't helpless after all. Maybe we all trip up sometime. When the car stopped outside my dark Victorian block it struck me that God had created a way of wiping out the consequences of all our actions, and us with them, painfully. What else was nuclear power for?

Peace Till the Moon Fails

Peace Till the Moon Fails

Maeve poured herself a second cup of coffee. Jeff never took any more than the one cup which he drank in gulps. He ate his whole dinner in a great hurry now that he did not talk much at meals. In the early years of their marriage they had brought to the table all the news and happenings of the day so that each would interest the other. 'Love, honour and entertain' should be the marriage vow, Jeff had said. His part of the entertainment had dwindled while the six children were at home, all intent on having their say and their mother's ear. Maeve had neglected him during that time but, as she said to herself, he was grown up and they were not. They needed her attention until they all left home and got married.

She lifted the evening paper although she would always have maintained that it was bad manners to read at the table. 'Oh goodness, Jeff,' she exclaimed. 'Oh dear.'

'What is it?' he said and she read out:

'The gardai are anxious to trace any relatives of Miss Winifred Teeling, found dead on Tuesday in her home at 56 Tobias Street. She had lived in Harp Buildings nearby

141

for forty years until she moved into her new home six weeks ago. None of the residents knew of any relatives although they said she was frequently away on visits. "She likes to keep herself to herself," they said.

'Her new neighbour, Mr Daniel O'Hagan, said, "She never spoke to me but I just glanced in her front window and I saw her lying on that green couch she had. I looked away quick but when I saw her there two mornings in a row I knocked on her door. There was no answer so I got the guards."

'She had enough food and fuel in the house. At the inquest the verdict was natural causes.'

'What's odd about all of that?' Jeff said.

'Miss Winifred Teeling – don't you remember? The awful woman who had our flat.'

'Oh God oh,' Jeff said, amused more than anything else.

'Of course I shouldn't say she was awful. I wasn't a bit nice to her.'

'She surely was awful,' Jeff said. 'Ask anybody around. Ask all the unfortunates that got her anonymous letters. A complete nutter and nasty with it. God, will I ever forget what it was like to have her hovering about up there, her big white face like a moon over the banisters. And you were miserable all the time she was in the house.'

'Oh I know I was,' Maeve agreed. 'But maybe it was my own fault. I didn't like her but if I had been nicer to her and chatted to her the way I do to anybody else she might have been all right.'

'Not at all,' Jeff said. 'It wouldn't have made the slightest difference. She was well set in her ways. I could see it. I would have hunted her only I didn't want to interfere in your arrangements.'

'The guards know she stayed here. After all, they took her away when you reported the letters. Will they come here to find out if I know of her family? I never found out anything about her. I never talked to her. Jeff, I'll be so ashamed.'

'They'll not bother their heads,' Jeff said. 'There won't be any record in the police station here and the ones down there won't know a thing about her. Anyway, they had the measure of her.'

'God forgive me,' Maeve said, 'but I was relieved to find that she was writing the letters. My first thought was that she could be made to leave. Then I was glad it was nobody we knew. I found myself looking at that poor woman who drinks, wondering could it possibly be her. I knew it wasn't somebody young because of the writing. I'd suspect any new people or the few women who had depressions. It really was very unpleasant to have such a thing in the district.'

'I never knew you were so upset by it,' Jeff said.

'She was looking forward to going into that house,' Maeve said. 'I didn't believe her about it. Why should she get a new house when families are in need?'

'These are little houses, specially built for old people,' Jeff said. 'They're lovely. They cost the city an absolute fortune. Maybe we'll apply for one ourselves.'

'I never want to leave here,' Maeve said. 'Oh I know you're only joking. But even though this house is too big for us now and hard to heat and keep clean, it has had the best part of my life in it. It comforts me.'

'What did we build the extension for?' Jeff asked. 'It was only in use for a few years. The clever people just bunged the children all in together and waited for them to move out. They might have gone sooner.'

'They went soon enough,' Maeve said. She often thought that Jeff did not miss their children as she did, that he was in

143

fact glad they were gone. As each engagement was announced she rejoiced in their happiness but the wrench of their leaving made her quarrel with them, made her carp at their arrangements so that she horrified herself. She never understood why she should have behaved in such a way. She only knew she missed the life they brought flowing through the house. 'I often felt I should apologise to Mary and Elizabeth for letting that woman into their room.'

'They were great friends in there,' Jeff said, smiling.

'They fought the piece out over who should clean it and how the space should be divided. Even though they had two wardrobes and two chests of drawers, it was such a mess while they were in it together. Once Mary left, Elizabeth kept it spotless. Wasn't I a fool to waste your money on turning it into a bed-sittingroom? I'd never risk letting it again, Jeff. You know that. I could not bear to.'

She cleared the table and they washed the few dishes. When he was at home he had always dried. The children had always had homework to do or somewhere to go. He had had a rota drawn up so that each child should help while he was away. He had thought she had to be protected from her demanding family.

When they were small she had decided that she would serve them, do what they wanted as far as possible, pick up for them, so that following her example they would serve one another and people generally. It did not quite seem to have worked. When she said to them, 'Maybe you would like to pick up your toys and put them in the press,' she found the room still littered and asked why. They explained, 'You said, Mammy, if we liked. But we didn't like.' She found it difficult to give them direct orders. She questioned her right to have their obedience. Perhaps they knew better than she did what made a comfortable sitting-room for them. She loved the things they said. She loved listening to them talking to one another.

She had had great plans when she fixed up the extension as a self-contained flat to let to a young girl. She had looked forward to the things she could do for her. She could offer her things she had cooked. She would have pointed out how difficult it was for her to cater for one while Jeff was away and it would be such a help if the girl would accept some. She'd give her little pots of marmalade or jam so that she would not have to depend on shop stuff. The girl would become like a daughter about the place. She would show Maeve dresses that she'd bought and come in saying things like, 'You'd never guess who I saw today,' and she'd tell about the daft sayings of the people who worked with her. They would all be known by their first names.

She had been deprived of all that for ever by Miss Teeling. She knew she had been victimised because of her unwillingness to put her foot down. Kindness had prevailed in letting the place to Miss Teeling but was not strong enough to make her be pleasant to her. Beforehand she had hated the emptiness of her home but it was bliss compared to the house with Miss Teeling squatting in it. She had joined clubs and societies to take her out but then she was nervous coming back in. The more she locked doors and windows the more nervous she became. She never mentioned this to Jeff. His job took him to Donegal from Monday to Thursday some weeks. She did not want him worrying about her. She knew he could not rearrange his life to suit her and she would have hated to be a burden.

When the dishes were cleared he said, as he often did, that he was going out to the pub. He would take one drink or two. Maeve read the newspapers.

'Who was there tonight?' she asked when he came back.

'The usual crowd,' he said and sat down in his armchair.

'I was thinking about Miss Teeling,' Maeve said. 'You know that big quartz stone we have on the window-ledge? She mentioned that the very first day she muscled in. She asked where we got it and I said at the seaside. I should have taken it away then. It was part of our family and I should not have left it where she was. I never liked her looking at it.'

'You weren't afraid she'd hit you with it?' Jeff laughed.

'Not at all,' Maeve said. 'I was never afraid of her like that. I wasn't ever afraid of her but I didn't like her or talk to her and she was always on my conscience – now even more so.'

'Do you remember finding that big stone?' Jeff smiled.

'Of course I do,' Maeve said. 'It was a cold windy day. We were on a big long beach in Donegal – Magheraroarty, wasn't it?'

'That's right,' Jeff said. 'We were in a wooden house that would have been more suited to the Austrian Alps. It creaked in the wind as if we were in a boat.'

'The children were so cross on the beach because the wind was stinging in from the sea. Gerry was shivering because he had forgotten his cap and his hood kept blowing off. They were supposed to be gathering shells but their fingers were blue. When they saw the dead sheep with its wool all sodden Monica began to cry and say everything was horrible. It changed when Mark found the stone. Every one of them cheered up, talking about it rolling round from Errigal mountain. They took turns carrying it to the car even though it was heavy for them. There wasn't a word of disagreement. Why did they love it, I wonder?'

'Well it's smooth and white and round. They liked the feel of it and the look of it, I suppose,' Jeff said.

'After each of those holidays I used to swear I'd never have another one,' Maeve said. 'If we had three or four good days that would be the limit. The rest of the time we'd drive round, with short walks and quick runs back to the car. We'd go into every craft shop along the coast of Ireland, where everybody would be steaming in wet clothes. But when the next summer was in sight I'd remember the times they sang in the car and lay in the sun. They would bring up talk about the currant loaves in Donegal or Lucey's Bakery in Waterville. And I'd look in the papers to rent another four-bedroomed seaside house with electricity and water.'

'They were a lot of work for you,' Jeff said. 'I always wished I could bring you to a good hotel.'

'I would not have wanted that,' Maeve said. 'I just wish it was possible to have a family holiday now. I would love to take Mary's family or Elizabeth's to the seaside and let them have time to draw breath.'

'There is no question of that,' Jeff said firmly. 'You are not going to kill yourself like that. Anyway, we're not young any longer. We deserve a bit of peace.'

'But you get on great with your grandchildren,' Maeve protested. 'They love when you play with them.'

'That's fine,' Jeff said. 'Kick a ball about, throw the little ones up in the air, ask them a few riddles. I can deal with that any day. But I am not having you slaving after them. You get tired. You know you do.'

Maeve gave up and went on to bed. Jeff filled her hot-water bottle, locked the doors, stoked the range and climbed the stairs while Maeve was in bed reading her book. It was a benefit of his being at home that she appreciated. She felt out of place looking after the night jobs around the house. When he opened the bedroom blinds a full moon was shining in. He hesitated. 'Will that moon keep you awake? Will I close over the blinds?'

'Oh no,' Maeve said. 'Isn't it lovely! In a clear, clear sky.' Then she remembered. 'I wish you hadn't compared Miss

Teeling's face to a moon over the banisters. I'll be thinking of her.'

Jeff laughed. 'I can't foresee all the strange thoughts you'll have.'

She was dropping off to sleep when she sat up suddenly. 'Goodness, Jeff. Suppose she had died here. What would we have done? It's not so long since she was here. How long is it, Jeff? If she died suddenly there, she could have died here. I would have felt her haunting this house for evermore. We would have had to leave.'

'She did not die here. Thank God for that. Now, Maeve, will you give yourself peace.'

She smiled. 'Peace till the moon fails.' The moonlight extended the sky to infinity. She could see Jeff's head flung back on the pillow. He had a big head, a big dark head and a dark chin. He used to shave every night before coming to bed. He was still a handsome man, she thought. She could not really remember what he had looked like when they were young. She was glad he had passed on his good looks to his six upstanding sons and daughters. And his decided way of looking at things. He never tortured himself over what he should do. He had such confidence. She smiled again. She remembered another line of the psalm: 'In his days justice shall flourish and peace till the moon fails.'